THE MARRIAGE
QUEST

THE MARRIAGE QUEST

BY

HELEN BROOKS

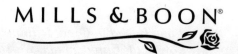

First published in Great Britain 1999
Large Print edition 1999
Harlequin Mills & Boon Limited,
Eton House, 18-24 Paradise Road,
Richmond, Surrey TW9 1SR

© Helen Brooks 1999

ISBN 0 263 16204 4

Set in Times Roman 16 on 17 pt
16-9910-57809 C1

Printed and bound in Great Britain
by Antony Rowe Ltd, Chippenham, Wiltshire

CHAPTER ONE

HENRIETTA heard the knock on the front door with a mixture of surprise and disbelief, and it was only Murphy lifting his massive head and growling softly deep in his throat that convinced her she hadn't imagined it.

'Good boy, Murphy.' She rose quickly, her eyes shooting to her wristwatch and then to the dark November sky outside the window. Ten o'clock. She never had any visitors at the best of times, but ten o'clock on a wild, windy November evening?

She hurried down the winding, bare wood stairs to the ground floor of the thirteenth-century converted water mill, and then paused in the small stone-flagged square of the hall, her hand going to Murphy's thick wide leather collar as the knock came again. She pulled Murphy close to her legs and opened the door whilst keeping the chain on.

'Yes?' As Henrietta peered through the crack Murphy kept up a steady rumbling, his sharp white teeth slightly bared, and she blessed him for it. 'Who's there?'

'Miss Noake?' It was a male voice, deep and throaty, but Henrietta still couldn't see more than a big shape in the dim light from the sixty-watt bulb behind her. 'Miss Henrietta Noake?'

'Yes.' She didn't like this, she didn't like it at all, Henrietta thought nervously, and then she found herself giving a squeal of fright as there was a thud and a crash outside and the door jerked and strained on the chain.

He had fallen. Whoever it was outside, he'd fallen, she thought in the split second before she said, 'What's happened? Are you all right?' to the mound on the floor. There was no reply.

She glanced down at Murphy, who returned the look enquiringly. The huge German shepherd was obviously as surprised by the turn of events as she was, Henrietta thought helplessly, but he had stopped growling. Whether that meant he had surmised any danger was past, or had concluded she was now going to shut the door and end the incident, she wasn't sure. But the figure on the floor wasn't moving, and there was no way she could just leave him there—whoever he was.

She had to push hard in order to close the door to take the chain off, and before she opened it again she reached for the baseball bat she kept in the hallstand for just such an emergency. She felt a bit silly, she admitted silently as she took a deep breath and opened the door, Murphy pressing protectively against her legs, but she'd rather feel silly than end up mugged or worse.

The man was big, very big, and liberally covered in mud and—this last she noticed with a thudding heart—blood. And he was still inert.

Henrietta prodded him gently with her foot. It wasn't exactly along the lines of the Good Samaritan, she chided herself reprovingly, before her more cautious self cut in with, But he's a darn sight bigger and heavier than you, Hen— and reassured her. He didn't stir under the prodding, and when Murphy sniffed round him and then nudged a limp arm with his big black nose she assumed the collapse was genuine. On first sight, Murphy resembled an enormous, thickly coated wolf rather than a domestic dog, and she doubted if anyone could play dead with those deadly jaws an inch or so away from their face.

She put the bat down before opening the door fully and stepping outside, kneeling at the side of the unconscious giant of a man and keeping her voice soft as she said, 'Can you hear me? Please, try and open your eyes.'

He was very attractive. It probably wasn't the moment to notice such a thing, but Henrietta couldn't help it. The dark, very masculine face was too rugged to be called handsome, but the thick black eyebrows, strong aquiline nose and well-shaped lips under the shock of jet-black hair combined to give looks that were more than a little arresting.

And then he groaned slightly, and a pair of piercingly blue eyes opened to stare straight into her soft brown ones, and the shock of it caused her to lose her balance and go sprawling backwards in an undignified scramble of arms and legs.

She was on her feet almost before her bottom had hit the ground, reassuring Murphy—who hadn't liked his mistress's fright and was being somewhat vocal to the instigator of it—before she leant over the stranger again and said, as calmly as she could, 'It's all right, you passed out, that's all. Do you think you can manage to get inside? It's starting to rain.'

'Hell…' When he tried to move Henrietta thought he was going to faint again, but he brushed aside her helping hand without allowing another groan to pass his white lips and dragged himself to his feet, using the stanchion of the door, levering himself into the hall before sinking down on to the bottom step of the stairs, his teeth clenched in pain.

'You've had an accident.' Too late she realised that as an observation it couldn't be more inane, but he merely nodded, breathing heavily for a few moments before he said briefly, 'Pheasant spooked my horse and he threw me.'

'Right.' She nodded in what she hoped was a capable, brisk fashion, and then, as he leant back against the side of the wall and closed his eyes, added, 'Brandy. A glass of brandy will help,' her voice high and anxious.

'Thanks, but you'd better make it a strong coffee,' he said flatly without opening his eyes. 'I think my leg is broken and I've had a whack on the head that would have felled an ox. If they need to operate on my leg it'd be better without alcohol in my system.'

'Oh, yes, of course.' Henrietta glanced now at the leg which was stretched straight out in front of him, and was appalled to notice that it was at a horribly awkward angle.

'It's not as bad as it looks.' He'd opened his eyes and seen her face and his voice was dry; in fact if the situation had been different she'd have sworn there was a touch of dark humour in the deep, husky tones. 'But it might be a good idea to phone the emergency services and get them to send an ambulance before you make that coffee?' he suggested imperturbably.

'Yes, yes, I'll do that now. The phone is upstairs. Will you be all right…?' Her voice trailed
away as the rivetingly blue eyes fastened fully
on hers and told her she was panicking.

'I'll be fine.' And then he smiled and she felt
as though she had been hit by a blinding bolt of
electricity as the hard face mellowed and softened. 'You just make the call.'

Murphy seemed to have assumed the role of
guard dog, his intelligent brown eyes fixed on
the cause of his mistress's unease and his big,
powerful body seated a foot or so away from
the bottom of the stairs as though to say, One
move towards her, mate, just one, and I'm having you.

Henrietta left him there after one attempt to
get him to go along with her which he patently
ignored, and, after stepping gingerly past the figure on the bottom step, flew upstairs to the first
floor of the three-storey building. In making the
call she realised how little she knew about the
stranger downstairs—she hadn't even asked his
name—but the ambulance was promised within
fifteen minutes, and she scurried downstairs
again to see if she could do anything for the
patient.

He was sitting exactly as she had left him—
Murphy still stolidly on duty in front of him—

and he looked even worse if anything. The dirt-engrained cut on his forehead was oozing blood, and his jacket and what she could see of his shirt underneath was a deep red.

'You're bleeding.' As soon as she had said it she wondered if she was destined to for ever make a fool of herself by stating the obvious with this man.

'My fault.' He raked back a lock of black hair wearily. 'I was feeling about with my hands, inspecting the damage, and I started it off again. Don't worry about it.'

But she did worry. It was nasty and it was deep, and he'd clearly already lost a considerable amount of blood. However, she nodded non-committally, walking into the kitchen and switching on the kettle before she made a wad of tissues into a thick pad, dabbed on a little antiseptic, and took them back to him. 'Press this on the wound while I get you that drink,' she said gently as he opened his eyes at her footsteps. 'The ambulance will be here in a few minutes but I'm afraid Friar's Mill is in the middle of nowhere, and there's half a mile of un-made road for it to get down before it reaches here.'

He inclined his head as he took the makeshift compress but said nothing, and Henrietta found

herself gabbling as she stood in front of him—
and it wasn't altogether due to worries about his
injuries, she admitted to herself wryly. He was
magnificent—even hurt and weak as he undoubtedly was. Quite what it was she wasn't
sure, but if it could be bottled and sold it would
make a million dollars.

'You say your horse threw you?' she asked
after a minute or two of reassuring him he was
going to be perfectly all right. The devastating
blue gaze had begun to glaze over and she had
purposely taken a hold of herself and her
tongue. 'You're a local, then?'

'Yes, I'm a local.' There was a flicker of the
former smile and then he said, his voice quiet,
'And you're renting the Mill for a time, I understand?'

For a moment her brow wrinkled, and then
she upbraided herself for her stupidity. Of
course, being a local, he would know she was a
townie—as any newcomer to this part of
Herefordshire was dubbed by the friendly village community some two or three miles away.
She had learnt on her arrival in these parts, some
nine months ago, that everyone knew everything
about *everyone*—it was the very antithesis of the
city life she had always been used to.

But with all the dark memories she had been trying to leave behind, and the devastating pain that had been with her day and night in the early days, she had purposely isolated herself from any contact with the villagers, politely but firmly refusing the invitations to fêtes and bazaars and barn dances that had come her way.

'I've taken a three-year lease.' She nodded at him as she spoke but proffered nothing more.

'Isn't it a little lonely out here by yourself?' he asked quietly as she turned to go towards the kitchen again.

'I'm not by myself.' She didn't turn round or check her exit. 'Murphy's here.'

So the dog was her only companion. The blue eyes narrowed thoughtfully. What had made a lovely young woman—and she *was* lovely, he acknowledged silently, in a quiet, innocent, even serene sort of way, with her great brown eyes and thick plait of hair—what had made her into a recluse at so young an age? There was a mystery here, and he rather liked the idea of unravelling it now he had the time. Perhaps he should have called on Miss Henrietta Noake before this?

'I decided on tea. Hot, sweet tea for shock.' He was brought out of his musings to find her standing in front of him again, her eyes wide and serious and her mouth straight.

'Thank you.' He took the mug gravely, noticing as he did so that she had a sprinkling of freckles across her nose that went well with the deep chestnut hair. Quite why he found the freckles sexy he didn't know—he had never done so before on other women, and this one wasn't at all the type he usually went for.

'Where's your horse?' Henrietta asked suddenly.

'What?'

He was taken aback and she found she was blushing wildly as the amused eyes met hers. 'Your horse?' she repeated awkwardly, feeling an absolute fool. 'You said your horse had thrown you.'

'Ah, yes.'

He was studying her in a way Henrietta didn't like, although she couldn't put her finger on why, but as the sky-blue eyes meandered over her face and hair she felt her cheeks grow even hotter. She was uncomfortably aware of a smidgen of dark body hair below his collar bone where the button of his shirt had come off in the fall, and the overall bigness of him, added to the virile masculinity that was positively tangible, was somehow…threatening. The word brought her up sharply and she recoiled from it—and him—stepping back a pace as her shoulders straightened.

He noticed the body language and lowered his gaze to the mug of tea as he answered, his voice soothing, 'I would imagine Ebony is back home in his stable by now; he's no fool. Unlike his master,' he added ruefully. 'He's still quite young but I thought I could handle his unpredictability and restlessness, and it was a good day for a gallop. Mind you, we were doing fine until that damn bird rose up under his hooves and scared the life out of him.'

'How long have you been out there?' Henrietta asked carefully, forcing her voice to sound normal.

'Well, I was out of it for a time, but when I came round it must have been about five.' He shook his head slowly, wincing as he did so and shifting his position slightly on the stairs. 'I was bang slap in the middle of nowhere, so I took stock and decided this was the nearest habitation if I could get to it, but as it meant crawling most of the way it took some time.'

'You must have people who are worried about you?' She stared at him as the thought occurred to her. 'I can phone and let them know you're all right if you'd like me to?'

'They're probably out looking,' he agreed easily, 'but I think I can hear the ambulance.' He was right; so could she. 'I'll get the hospital to do all the necessary legwork; don't worry about it.'

'Oh, but it's no trouble—'

'And thank you, Henrietta,' he cut in softly, 'for being a ministering angel. I'd like to give you a call when this—' he gestured to his injured leg '—is sorted. We could perhaps go out for a drink or a meal?'

'No.' It was too sharp and too instinctive, and as the colour surged back into her face with renewed vigour Henrietta tried desperately to backtrack. 'No, thank you very much, but that's really not necessary,' she said feverishly. 'Anyone would have done the same and I only made a phone call. You don't need to feel obligated.'

'I don't.' He smiled, but it didn't reach the devastating blue eyes this time. 'I merely wanted the pleasure of your company for an evening, that's all. Or perhaps your social life is too hectic at the moment? I can leave it a week or two if you like?'

She wasn't going to be manipulated or forced into doing anything she didn't want to. *Never*, in all her life, was she going to let that happen again, Henrietta told herself flatly as a flood of icy-cold reality doused the hot agitation and panic. And now the words came easily as she said, her voice cool and firm, 'It's not that I'm too busy, but I don't go out at all, not in the evenings.'

'You mean you don't date.' It was a statement, not a question, and one that required no comment from her. 'I'm sorry about that, Henrietta Noake,' he said thoughtfully. 'Very sorry.'

'Don't be.' She smiled brightly, clicking her fingers at Murphy as the wail of the ambulance ceased and the scrunching of footsteps sounded outside. 'I'm perfectly happy as I am, thank you.'

'It wasn't you I was sorry for,' he said cryptically, but then further conversation was swallowed up by the knock at the front door and the subsequent furore of the two burly, brisk ambulancemen asking the necessary questions before transporting their patient into the back of the waiting vehicle.

Her last sight of the big figure, as she stood outside in the drizzling rain and watched them close the back of the ambulance, was a lazy hand raised in farewell and a white face that belied the smiling mouth. He'd got some guts and an iron control, Henrietta thought grudgingly as she nodded her farewell to the two ambulancemen. She had seen the look that had passed between them when one of them had inspected their patient's leg. It was a painful injury, there was no doubt about that, and their incredulity when he had told them the circumstances of the accident and his subsequent crawl to the mill had spoken for itself.

But she didn't want to see him again. There was absolutely no doubt in Henrietta's mind as she watched the big vehicle swing round, and begin the ascent up the gravelly track towards the main road some half a mile away. In fact, she couldn't think of anyone she wanted to see less than him. He was too unsettling, too… Her mind searched for an adequate description to explain her alarm and unease and failed, causing her to shrug her shoulders as the tail-lights of the ambulance disappeared and the deep, seething blackness of the windy dark night took over again. It didn't matter anyway. The incident was done with, finished.

She glanced down at Murphy, standing like a sentinel at her side, and stroked the massive head absently before turning towards the warmth and light of the house.

*   *   *

It was just after lunch the next day when Henrietta was busy in the kitchen washing up her dish and Murphy's bowl—the pair of them having shared a pan of home-made vegetable soup and fresh crusty rolls—rather than being ensconced in her studio in the annexe at the back of the mill, that she heard the sound of a car making its way down the track outside, followed a few seconds later by a knock at the door.

What now? She hastily dried her hands and with Murphy hot at her heels walked through to the hall and opened the door.

'Miss Noake?' The delivery boy was fresh-faced and smiling, and almost hidden by the enormous bouquet he was holding.

'Yes, but these can't possibly be for me,' Henrietta began in a bewildered tone, before realisation dawned—her visitor of the night before.

She took the flowers from the boy, whose smile had dimmed somewhat on his sight of Murphy, and after thanking him closed the door.

There were a hundred or more deep red roses in the bouquet along with white and delicately tinted yellow lilies, sweet-smelling freesias and a mass of feathery baby's breath, but it was the accompanying card that disturbed Henrietta the most. It wasn't written by a woman's hand, and the bold black scrawl could only belong to one person, she thought shakily. 'I rarely take no for an answer,' he had written arrogantly, 'and I would still like to take you out for that meal some time, but for now these flowers will have to serve to remind you of me now and again.' There was no signature, which only emphasised how little she knew about him, whereas he knew her name, where she lived, *everything*.

'No, he doesn't; of course he doesn't,' Henrietta muttered to herself as she carried the flowers through to the kitchen and then stood looking at the bouquet on the kitchen table without making a move to unwrap it. In fact, he knew no more about her than anyone in the village; she mustn't let her imagination run away with her here. And the fact that he had written the card himself, instead of allowing a shop assistant to do it, didn't mean anything either.

He was grateful, that was all, she told herself firmly, staring warily at the flowers as though they were going to bite her. He had been in a terrible predicament last night, and if she hadn't been at home, or hadn't heard his knock, the outcome could have been very serious, even fatal, because the night had been a cold, wet one.

And if he called to see her again when he was on his feet—her heart began to thud uncomfortably at the possibility—or rang her, she would tell him, politely but unwaveringly, that she had meant what she'd said last night and that he was wasting his time. She nodded briskly to herself and then smiled down at Murphy who, sensing her turmoil, had begun to whine plaintively.

'It's all right, boy.' She went down on her knees and hugged the broad neck as a large pink tongue washed her cheek. 'We know what we're doing, don't we? Now, how about a biscuit or two for dessert before we start work again, eh?'

And she would see to the flowers later. As she rose to her feet again, Henrietta's soft brown eyes hardened. Her days of dancing to a man's tune—any man's tune—were over. She was on her own now, and contrary to what the sender of the bouquet might think, or anyone else for that matter, she loved, *relished*, every minute of her independence, and she would never give it up.

CHAPTER TWO

November passed and December arrived in a medley of sparkling white frosts that had Henrietta lighting the wood-burning stove in her living quarters on the first floor before she even dressed in the mornings. It was bitterly cold, but days spent in the studio at her pottery and painting, and cosy evenings in front of the roaring stove with Murphy at her feet and the wind howling outside, were not unpleasant and Henrietta was content. Except…

She frowned now, her thoughts wandering as she fixed a plateful of bacon rind and bread to scatter outside on the makeshift bird table she had constructed in the summer. The old mill was built on a small incline that overlooked the River Arrow, and in the warmer months the river had been alive with curlews, goldfinches, chaffinches, linnets, willow warblers and kingfishers, with two herons and a peregrine falcon making the odd visit first thing in the morning and owls and bats claiming the territory at night.

Now Henrietta only had the dried flowers hanging in the kitchen as a reminder of those hot days, but the birds were around, along with a resident otter or two and a den of badgers a couple of fields away.

But Henrietta wasn't thinking of wildlife as her hands became still and she stared vacantly out of the kitchen window to the tumbling river beyond—or not the furry and feathered kind at least.

After the bouquet, which must have cost him a small fortune, she had fully expected her night visitor to be in touch either by phone or a personal appearance, but the weeks had stretched and lengthened and now it was the middle of December and she still hadn't heard anything.

Not that she wanted to, she reminded herself sharply as her frown deepened. Of course she didn't—that was the last thing she wanted—but it was just that she would have liked to know he was all right, that he'd recovered from that nasty injury to his leg. It sounded feeble even to her own ears, and she shook herself crossly, making an impatient sound deep in her throat.

Far better to let sleeping dogs lie. The intervening weeks had dulled her recollection of how she had felt on that night, but if she started to meditate on it for any length of time her heart began to thud and that same sense of panic and agitation made her hands damp. He was dan-

gerous somehow, that man. And she made no
apology for the dramatic thought, she added
stoutly. If you were tempted to play with fire
you ran the risk of getting burnt, and she had
enough scar tissue to last her a lifetime…

Murphy's gentle nudge against her legs reminded her he was waiting for his bacon titbit
from the plate before she went outside to the
bird table, and she came back to normality with
a rush of love and gratitude towards the big animal whose demands for love and companionship and looking after had kept her going at the
beginning of the year when nothing else could
have.

The phone call came just as it was beginning to
get dark, when she and Murphy were cleaning
themselves up after a winter's walk along the
river bank. The surrounding countryside was a
doggy haven, with hundreds of smells to follow,
rivers to swim in, sticks to chase and mud to
wallow in, but inevitably it meant a big clean-
up operation once they were back at the mill,
and this day was no exception.

Henrietta left Murphy on his blanket in the
kitchen and ran up to her living quarters on the
first floor, but once there she hesitated in lifting
the receiver. It was him—she knew it was him.

Of course it could have been her mother, or her brother and his family, or any one of a number of friends she still kept in touch with by letter and phone from her old life in London, but she knew, somehow, it was him.

The phone continued to ring, and at last she took hold of herself and picked up the receiver with a tentative hand. 'Hello?' Her voice was too weak and she heard it with a healthy burst of self-contempt. What was the matter with her, for goodness' sake?

'Henrietta?'

It was the deep, slightly husky and very male voice that had haunted her dreams for the last five weeks, and she gulped deep in her throat before she managed, 'Yes?'

'How are you?' It was dark and almost amused, as though he could sense her discomfiture, and everything in Henrietta immediately rebelled.

'Who is this?' She knew exactly who it was but she wasn't going to give him the satisfaction of knowing that. She had the notion that this particular male ego was quite big enough as it was, she thought testily.

'You gave me comfort and sustenance a few weeks ago,' he said softly. 'Do you remember?

Or do you often take needy men to your bosom?' he added silkily.

It was deliberately provocative but she still couldn't help rising to the bait. 'I hardly took you to my bosom,' she said as frostily as she could manage through the tantalising image his words had conjured up. 'I made a phone call and gave you a cup of tea as I remember.'

'Just so.' And to her chagrin he was speaking soothingly, in the sort of tone one used when dealing with a difficult and recalcitrant child.

Henrietta gritted her teeth. This was getting ridiculous, she thought irritably. She took a deep breath, counted to ten, then asked as calmly and sweetly as she could, 'How are you feeling now, Mr…?'

'My leg is much better,' the deep voice announced cheerfully, 'although I'll need a bit of physiotherapy. That's why I'm ringing.'

'I'm sorry?'

'To arrange that meal we spoke of?' The tone suggested it was a foregone conclusion. 'I'm not into hobbling around on crutches—' no, she could imagine that would have spoilt the macho-man image, Henrietta thought nastily '—but another week and I'll be back in the swing. I know Christmas is a busy time for everyone, but if you tell me what dates you have free we'll go from there,' he concluded helpfully.

'Dates?' She stared at the phone for a moment and willed herself to remain calm. 'Look, I'm sorry, Mr...?' The pause continued for so long she was forced to say, 'But I thought I made it perfectly clear on that night a few weeks ago. I don't accept invitations from strangers.' Straight speaking was clearly all that would get through that thick skin.

'If you came out with me I wouldn't be a stranger, would I?' he suggested reasonably. 'Problem solved. And any way, you nursed my wounds and provided comfort; that makes me more of a friend than a stranger.'

She didn't like the way he said 'nursed my wounds and provided comfort' in that soft, smoky kind of voice, and she bit her tongue, willing her voice not to tremble and ignoring the warm flutter in her stomach the velvet tones had produced as she said, 'No, I'm sorry. You're very kind, but I would rather not.'

'I thought it was me, but you give the brush-off to everyone, don't you?' he said thoughtfully after a full ten seconds had crept by and Henrietta's nerves were screaming.

'I beg your pardon?' She couldn't believe her ears.

'You're the original mystery woman in the village, do you know that?' he continued conversationally, totally ignoring the sharp outrage in her voice. 'You've had the odd visitor now and again—a tall, red-haired woman for one who looks so much like you everyone has assumed it's your mother—' how dared they? How dared they spy on her like that, Henrietta asked herself furiously, and, worse, how dared he *tell* her? '—but you haven't responded to one overture of friendship or got involved in any area of village life. Now, that's not normal.'

'*Not normal?*' She was screeching but she didn't care.

'Not by a long chalk.' He sounded as if he was enjoying himself. 'You're a young woman of—what? Twenty-two, twenty-three? And you live alone with the Hound of the Baskervilles, making your pots and painting your pictures, or whatever it is you do in that lonely old mill. Now, you can't blame people for being curious, can you?'

'Yes, I darn well can!' She was so mad she could hardly get the words out. 'I happen to have my own pottery business if you must know, and it provides me with a living; it's a *job*!' She literally spat the last three words out. 'And I sell my paintings too; that's part of my career, my livelihood. It's not some quaint little hobby, whatever you and the rest of the gossips think. And any work of this nature is best done in peace and quiet which makes the mill ideal, not that I have to explain anything to you.'

'Where do you sell your work? Not in the village.' There was an element of what sounded like disbelief in his tone, and it wasn't until much later, and after two fortifying gin and tonics, that Henrietta realised she had been drawn out by a master of manipulation. And by then it was far, far too late.

'No, not in the village,' she snapped back tightly. 'As it happens my mother and my brother own a shop and a small art gallery in London, and they sell my work there. And not because they are family,' she added sharply, as though he had voiced that very thought, 'but because my work is good enough to be sold. They are business people first and foremost, and my brother is also my agent.'

'I see.' It was meek. 'But why come all the way to Herefordshire when you sell your work in London? Wouldn't it make more sense to rent somewhere closer to where the trade is and where it's all happening?'

'I used to live close—' Henrietta stopped abruptly, the words strangling in her throat as a picture of the airy flat she had shared with Melvyn flashed over the screen of her mind. 'Look, I don't want to discuss this any further,' she said shakily, screwing up her eyes tight as she struggled to keep the darkness out of her voice. 'And I have to go now, I'm sorry.'

'Okay.' He was suspiciously amenable all of a sudden. 'But if you won't come out with me you really ought to try and meet a few more people, Henrietta. It's not healthy for you to lock yourself away like you do, and the people round here aren't so bad once you get to know them. You've hurt a few feelings, you know,' he added sorrowfully.

He made her feel as though she was the worst person on the planet. 'No, I haven't.' The self-defence was instinctive. 'Name one.'

'Me.' And then the phone went dead.

'Huh.' She remained standing exactly as she was as she glared at the receiver in her hand for a full minute more, and she really didn't know if she wanted to burst into tears or throw the phone at the wall. In the end she did neither, merely replacing the receiver with elaborate gentleness before walking across to the old oak dresser in a corner of the room and pouring herself a generous gin and tonic from her small store of alcohol in the bottom cupboard.

The cheek of the man. The *cheek* of the man. She was shaking, she realised as she raised the glass to her lips and took a long, trembling gulp. How dared he criticise her like that—make her out to be some sort of oddity just because she hadn't gone to their endless fêtes and bazaars and barn dances and such? Anyone would think it was written into the deeds of this place that you had to associate with all and sundry if you took up residence.

She finished the drink and refilled the glass before walking over to the big comfy sofa in front of the wood-burning stove, and, after throwing a couple more logs on the fire, sank down into the sofa's well-padded depths.

They had no idea how desperate she had been in February when she had first come here, Henrietta thought numbly. Desperate, ridden with guilt, unable to sleep or eat... And it had all been so different just two years before when she had married Melvyn on her twenty-third birthday. She had thought the world was their oyster then, that the two of them were going to have an enchanted life, a fairy-tale existence.

She had met Melvyn through her brother and even then, at the young age of twenty-six, his sculptures were already being acclaimed as brilliant. And he *had* been brilliant, Henrietta ad-

mitted fairly. Brilliant, wild and utterly capti-
vating, with his dark, flashing eyes and thick
shock of black hair he wore long in a ponytail.
He'd been a genius. A mad genius. Although
no, that wasn't quite fair, she qualified wearily.
He'd been sane in every respect other than his
obsession with her, and that was what his love
had been—obsessional. If only she had realised
it sooner, before they had married.

But he had swept her off her feet and they
had met and married within three months, and
she'd thought she was the luckiest girl in the
world as she had walked down the aisle. And
within a few weeks she had found herself in a
living hell.

He had breathed her, slept her, eaten and
drunk her, wanting to be with her every moment
of the day and night, controlling her work, her
mind, her thoughts until she thought she was
going insane. His love had been suffocating and
of a nature that was unexplainable to the average mind. His fits of jealousy if she should so
much as glance at another man had been frightening, his cutting off of all her friends and people from her life before him absolute. She hadn't
realised what he was doing at first, and then,
when it had dawned on her why she was be-

coming more and more isolated, she had fought back as best she could.

But he had been a Jekyll and Hyde character—her wonderful, kind, loving, passionate Melvyn one minute, and a fiend the next, twisting everything round until she had begun to believe it was her that was at fault most of the time.

He had slowly undermined her confidence in herself and her work as he had strengthened the cords of guilt and fear holding her to him until all her love for him was gone, swallowed up in the constant turmoil and confusion. But she hadn't realised it, so great had been her bewilderment and so consuming the vacuum she had been pushed into. She had just known she was becoming dependent on him for her next breath, her next thought, and it had terrified her.

But to her mother and her brother and those of his friends they still saw he had appeared the perfect husband, attentive, loving, catering for her every need. And he *had* loved her in his own way, Henrietta thought now as she hugged herself round her middle, swaying back and forth in an agony of remembrance. But it was an unnatural love, grotesque and distorted, a love that wanted to consume the object of its devotion until there was nothing left.

In the last few months they had been together she had wished him gone. The guilt rushed over her again, thick and heavy. He had told her he would never let her go, that she was his for ever, that nothing would part them. He had even said he would rather kill her and himself than let her go, and she'd believed him. But then he had told her about the appointment he had made for her to be sterilised so that no third party, no child, would ever come between them, and the full enormity of what had happened—what she had *let* happen—over the last months had really hit her.

She had sought help, tried to make her mother and her brother understand, visited the doctor, cried out in the only way she knew how, but Melvyn was clever and she doubted if anyone, even now, really understood.

And then, that fateful night, they had had their last quarrel. It had started through her refusal to agree to the operation he had pressed for, but when she had stuck her heels in and rejected all his arguments he had become violent, and she had really feared for her life. She had run out of the flat and Melvyn had followed, catching her up at the corner of the street and metamorphosing into that other man, the man she'd thought she had married.

They had been walking home when the stolen car, driven by underage youths high on drugs, had mounted the pavement, and Melvyn had turned and seen the car almost upon them. He could have jumped out of the way—that was the thing that still haunted her and woke her up in the night in a cold sweat—he could have, but he didn't. Instead he'd used the split second it took for the car to reach them to push her out of the way, knowing there was no time for him to save himself too. In the final analysis he had given his life for her...

'Don't think about it.' She spoke the words out loud, jumping up from the sofa as she did so. She had thought about nothing else in the dreadful aftermath of the accident, and she had nearly gone mad with guilt after she had acknowledged that if she could have had him back—for their old life to resume—she wouldn't. Not that she wanted him dead, she'd told herself over and over again, but just out of her life—somewhere else. Anywhere else. But not dead. Not that.

Murphy's reproachful eyes told her she was late with his dinner when she walked into the kitchen a few moments later, and again she blessed the huge animal for the diversion from her thoughts. And as she busied herself with his meat and biscuits—the pit at the end of the kitchen where the old inner millstone had once rumbled slightly spooky in the shadows—she reaffirmed the vow she had made months before. Murphy and her work were everything now, and that was the way it was going to remain. She never wanted another man in her life, not now and not in the future, and no sweet-talking charmer with piercing blue eyes and a smile to kill for was going to make her change her mind either.

She nodded to herself, placing the dog bowl on the stone-slabbed floor and watching Murphy as he gobbled down his dinner with indecent haste. Whatever the temptation, you didn't willingly step into hell twice in one lifetime.

However, Henrietta had to admit to herself that it was the result of the phone call that made her accept the invitation from the Vincent estate when it came the next morning. The mill and hundreds of acres of surrounding green countryside were all owned by the Vincents—or one particular Vincent, she understood, who had inherited the estate from his late father but who chose to live abroad most of the year.

Apparently, so Henrietta learnt from the village shopkeeper when she drove in to collect her groceries that same day, the Vincent estate always gave a Christmas party for their employees and the villagers. It was a tradition dating back a couple of centuries, and one which the present owner, Jared Vincent, had continued in spite of his self-imposed virtual exile from England.

'You thinking of going, then, m'dear?' the stout, motherly shopkeeper asked when Henrietta explained she had received an invitation too. 'My hubby and me'll be going; you can come along with us if you're a bit nervous, like.'

'That's very nice of you.' Henrietta was touched by the offer, especially as she'd had to admit, when she'd thought about it the night before, that she *had* been somewhat stand-offish with the community hereabouts. And so her presence at the party ten days hence—on December the twenty-third—was settled.

CHAPTER THREE

'Wow…' The comment was merely the faintest breath of a sigh, but Mrs Baker heard it anyway and turned round in the front seat of the car to look at Henrietta.

'Impressive, isn't it?' she agreed with an air of satisfaction.

Fotheringham Hall *was* impressive. As the Bakers' old Escort travelled sedately along the winding drive to the huge stately home in the distance, Henrietta peered out of the side window at the discreetly lit mansion silhouetted against the night sky and wondered if the simple, short, crushed-velvet evening dress she had on was elegant enough for such surroundings.

It served to take her mind away from the other thought that had been with her all day— or ever since she had received the invitation, if she were being honest, she corrected herself wryly. And that was whether *he* would be here tonight—whoever he was and whatever his name was.

She hoped he wasn't. Her bright-eyed, carefully coiffured reflection in the car window mocked the statement, and she found herself frowning as she reiterated the thought more strongly in the minute or two before the car drew to a halt in the massive, horseshoe-shaped forecourt. *She didn't want to see him; she didn't.*

They were ushered into the baronial hall by a stocky, amiable doorman who nevertheless inspected their gold-edged invitations carefully before he let them through. Henrietta was impressed. And even more so when, immediately the door closed behind them, a smart uniformed waiter appeared at their side with a tray of drinks and a bright smile.

'Always does us proud, does Mr Jared.' Mrs Baker had been born and bred in the village and considered herself one of the family. 'There's always enough food to feed an army, and dancing and such like. Of course, some folk don't know when they've had enough; that's why a lot of 'em have taxis tonight, but my Harold has never been one for the drink.'

Mr Baker's glance at Henrietta over the head of his wife stated quite clearly that he had never been given the chance, and Henrietta smiled at the little man—who was undoubtedly henpecked—sympathetically before she said quietly, 'Is Jared Vincent here tonight?'

'Oh, yes, dear, there he is. At the foot of the stairs.'

Oh, hell. As her gaze was met and held by that piercing blue one Henrietta knew that *he* knew she hadn't had the faintest idea of the identity of Jared Vincent before this moment.

Jared had stopped talking to the little group clustered around him as she had looked over, and now he leant back against the ornately carved wood of the banister without taking his eyes off her, folding his arms over his powerful chest as he watched her eyes widen in dismay. And then he smiled coolly, his lips twisting quizzically as he raised one hand in a brief salute before returning his attention to the tall blonde woman at his side.

She didn't believe this. Henrietta became aware that Mrs Baker was talking at the side of her and forced herself to concentrate on her self-appointed mentor. 'I'm sorry?' she said dazedly.

'I said it appeared as though you two knew each other.' Mrs Baker was ruffled and it showed. 'I thought you said you'd never met Mr Jared?'

'I didn't think I had.' Henrietta quickly related the circumstances of their meeting, but she could tell Mrs Baker was sceptical.

'And you didn't know it was Mr Jared?' she asked doubtfully.

As Henrietta was about to reply, a deep dark voice at the side of her said mockingly, 'Mr and Mrs Baker, how nice to see you, and I gather you're looking after my ministering angel for me?'

'Mr Jared...' Mrs Baker went all of a flutter, and it was some minutes later when Jared steered Henrietta to one side of the throng and looked down into her face from his great height.

He must be all of six foot six. That was the first thought that had registered on Henrietta's stunned mind during the discourse with the Bakers, closely followed by, And he's gorgeous. Dressed in muddy, blood-stained clothes he had been pretty amazing, but now, in a beautifully cut, dark grey lounge suit that sat on the big body with intimidating ease, he was overwhelming. His shirt and tie were exactly the same blue as his eyes and of the finest silk, if she wasn't much mistaken, but it was the overall flagrant masculinity that was paralysing her now. She had only known one other man who had possessed the sort of magnetic charisma Jared Vincent had, and there had been a dark, deadly side to the charm that had all but ruined her life.

'You look scared to death.' Like Melvyn, he
went straight for the jugular, Henrietta thought
helplessly. 'What have you heard about me to
make you look like that?' he asked softly.

'Heard?' She shook her head nervously. 'I
haven't heard anything, and of course I'm not
scared.' It didn't convince her so it certainly
wouldn't cut any ice with him, and she forced
her voice to sound firmer as she added, 'I
mustn't keep you from your other guests.'

'Damn my other guests.' It was still soft but
there was an element of steel under the silk now,
and it made the resemblance to Melvyn even
stronger. 'You came in here tonight smiling and
relaxed, and then you set eyes on me and you
looked like you were in the presence of the
Marquis de Sade. Now, I want to know why. As
far as I'm aware we'd never met before that
night some weeks ago. Is that right?'

She nodded warily. He had terribly thick
lashes for a man, and their blackness emphasised the brilliant blue of his eyes so that the
effect was riveting. It made it difficult even to
think about glancing away, she thought dazedly,
but she was blowed if she was going to stand
here and be interrogated. Her only crime was
helping him when he'd arrived on her doorstep,
and then refusing to take their association any

further. If his male ego couldn't take no for an answer it was tough.

'Look, Mr Vincent—'

'Jared,' he cut in smoothly. 'You've mopped my fevered brow so I think we can drop the formalities, don't you?'

He made the mopping of the fevered brow sound terribly intimate, she thought irritably. It was on the same lines as the phone call, and definitely flirtatious.

'And if it's not something you've heard, do I take it you've taken an instant dislike to me? Is that it?'

Now how on earth do you answer something like that? Henrietta stared at him in dismay. He was obviously a man who didn't go in for polite platitudes, but the last thing she could do was to reveal why she wanted nothing to do with men in general—and him in particular, she thought helplessly.

She decided to hide behind sarcasm. 'Are you so short of female company it would worry you if I had?' she asked quietly, her tone lightly mocking and her eyes expressive as she glanced over at the willowy blonde he had been conversing with when she had entered the house.

He followed her gaze and then brought his eyes back to her, and their blueness was hard

and unequivocally direct as he said, 'Well
fielded, my brown-eyed beauty, but I've side-
stepped a difficult issue too often myself not to
recognise the manoeuvre. So, you have no in-
tention of being drawn,' he added thoughtfully.

Henrietta continued to look at him but she
said nothing; there was nothing to say after all.

'Well, no problem.' He smiled suddenly and
she blinked at what it did to the rugged male
face. 'You are here tonight and I intend to make
sure you enjoy yourself; it's the least I can do.
Finish that—' he pointed at the glass of sherry
in her hand '—and we'll circulate for a while;
there's a few people you should meet before the
dancing starts.'

'I…I'm not going to stay that long.' It was a
spur-of-the-moment decision, but she had just
had the awful knowledge dawn on her con-
sciousness that this man, this determined, strong
and very male man, was her landlord, and not
only that but he was undeniably powerful and
wealthy.

And he had set her up with that telephone
call, she thought feverishly. All the prodding to
integrate with the community and make friends
had been a means to an end. He had *known* she
was going to receive his invitation the next day

and probably refuse it—he had been feeding her a guilt trip to make her accept.

'The Bakers always stay to the bitter end,' Jared said silkily, 'and you came with them, didn't you?'

'It doesn't mean I have to go home with them,' Henrietta countered quickly. 'I... I intended to get a taxi...' Her voice trailed away at the blatant scepticism on the hard face.

'Henrietta Noake, you disappoint me,' he said severely. 'I had you down as a rare thing in this wicked world of ours—a truthful and honourable female.'

The flush that her lie had already lent to her face deepened and she would have given the world to be able to say something rude. As it was she bit her tongue and forced her voice not to rise, her tone flat as she said, 'Did you indeed?'

'And I can't keep calling you Henrietta,' Jared murmured softly. 'It's one hell of a mouthful. You must have a shortened version your friends use?' he asked persuasively.

'Hen,' she said shortly.

'*Hen?*' It clearly wasn't to his liking. 'You let people call you Hen?' he asked incredulously, his eyes washing over the lovely face in front of him framed by a cloud of silky chestnut-red hair that fell in soft waves halfway down her back.

'Yes.' Henrietta found she was quite enjoying herself now; the blank astonishment on his face was rather gratifying.

'I see.' He frowned at her before taking hold of her arm, his touch burning her skin. 'Henrietta it is, then, until I can think of something more pleasing to us both.'

Oh, no. No, no, no. There was going to be no 'more pleasing to us both', she thought determinedly as she allowed him to lead her over to a small group at the far end of the hall. This evening was going to be a one-off, not-to-be-repeated experience, she told herself firmly, and she was probably going to hate every minute of it anyway. She had never liked aggressive, egotistical men at the best of times, and the only reason Jared Vincent was slightly interested in her was because she had given him the cold shoulder. It was so obvious, the more so now she knew who he was. He was used to having the women line up, no doubt; with his looks and position he didn't exactly have to beg for a date from anyone, and her repudiation of his advances had whetted his appetite; that was all it was. She was out of his league in every sense.

'Smile.'

'What?' The deep voice was very soft in her ear and for a moment she thought she had mis-heard him as they neared the others.

'I said smile.' The piercing eyes looked into hers as he halted, drawing her into the circle of his arms as he smiled slowly. 'That scowl on your face isn't exactly guaranteed to win friends and influence people,' he said softly.

Short of causing a scene there was no way she could extricate herself from his casual em-brace, but he was too close. Way, way too close. She forced herself to ignore the intoxicating smell of him and the feel of his hard-muscled arms around her waist, but she knew she had tensed and her face was straight when she said, 'Will you please let go of me, Mr Vincent?'

'No.' He didn't even pretend to acquiesce. 'No, I won't. Not until you call me Jared.'

He was dark and dangerously attractive, and again the raw, overwhelming maleness of him was tangible, causing a fluttering ache in her lower stomach that she despised herself for. She tried to pull herself together and look strict and assertive as she said, 'Your other guests are looking at us.'

'I couldn't care less.' He was obviously en-joying her discomfiture. 'Let them look.'

'I'll cause a fuss—'

'No, you won't,' he interrupted lazily. 'You are far too much of a lady to make an exhibition of yourself, or me for that matter.'

'But you're no gentleman,' she shot back angrily.

He smiled. A sexy, smoky smile that did incredible things to her nerve-endings. 'How clever of you to guess,' he said mildly. 'Now, are you going to co-operate?'

It was a *fait accompli*, and he was quite intimidating enough normally without her being pressed against that big, powerful frame that was evoking the sort of feelings she could have done without. Henrietta thought resignedly. However, it was one thing to have won a battle and quite another to have won the war.

'Will you let go of me…Jared?' His name was strange on her tongue. 'Is that all right?' she asked tartly. But the sharpness was forced.

'The content of the request is all wrong,' he murmured quietly, his eyes wicked, 'but in view of the fact that we are presently surrounded by a hundred pairs or so of interested eyes it perhaps is a moot point.'

'Well?' She was still enclosed within his arms and her voice was definitely confrontational, but Jared was finding the initial impulse he'd had of piercing that formidable barrier in order to make her notice him—really notice him—had now degenerated into something else. Something that was all mixed up with lustful desire and aching uncertainty, like a teenager on his first date. *Ridiculous*. The sapphire-blue eyes narrowed as he became disturbed by the realisation that he hadn't allowed a female to affect him like this since… Oh, he couldn't remember when.

'Forgive me, O virtuous one.' He was mocking himself more than her, but Henrietta didn't know that. She only knew he let go of her somewhat abruptly, his face changing, and for a moment or two she felt quite bereft and terribly alone.

But then in the next instant she was being introduced to one new face after another and all of them charming and *so* pleased to meet her—but then of course they would be, wouldn't they, Henrietta thought churlishly, if she was on the arm of Jared Vincent? He clearly had a considerable sway within this country community in spite of the fact that he lived abroad most of the time.

And it was that thought that prompted her to say, in the break between the last of the introductions and the beginning of the dancing, 'I understand you're away from England for a good part of the year? Have you other homes abroad?'

'In France and the States.' He was leaning back against the wall as he surveyed her lazily, a pose she felt was entirely natural to him. He was like one of the big cats, she thought warily. Cool, confident, with a lithe, prowling kind of male sensuality that was covertly menacing. 'But it's business that keeps me away most of the time. My grandfather was something of a whizkid for his time and upbringing, and he had the notion quite early in life that it wasn't enough to merely be a member of the British aristocracy and hunt and fish. Maybe he foresaw the horror of death duties and so on; I don't know. Anyway, he used some of the Vincent fortune to invest and speculate in France and the States, and he was a shrewd old bird.'

'You liked him,' she stated discerningly.

'Very much.' He smiled at her, the blue eyes crinkling at the corners. 'He was like one of the heroes from those spaghetti westerns, a loner who lived by his own set of values and princi-ples and who didn't know the meaning of the word compromise.'

'Do you?'

He didn't answer, and she pressed, 'Do you know the meaning of the word compromise, or are you your grandfather's disciple?'

He continued to regard her for a few moments more, his eyes sweeping over her uplifted chin and shadowed eyes, and then he said, his voice very soft, 'Why all the aggression, Henrietta? Who has hurt you so badly?'

'What?' She was so startled she actually took a step backwards before she recovered herself enough to force a smile and say, 'I don't know what you're talking about.'

'That word compromise touched a raw nerve, didn't it?' Jared said with frightening discernment as he straightened his big lean body and moved closer. And then, when she didn't answer but just stared at him, her mouth tight, he added, 'What was his name?'

She bitterly resented the way he was making her feel—like a small confused animal with nowhere to hide—and her anger came through in her voice when she said, 'If, *if* I had had some sort of difficult relationship as you are suggesting, that's my business and mine alone.'

'And you intend to keep it that way,' he stated quietly.

This was crazy! She had only met the man twice in her whole life and he expected her to pour out her life history? Her voice was level when she spoke out her thoughts and said, 'I don't know you so why on earth would I tell you anything intimate?'

It was the wrong word to use and she knew it at once, and her slip of the tongue was emphasised by the sudden glitter in his eyes and the slight quirking of one black eyebrow. 'Intimate…' He let the word trail over his tongue for as long as it took for her skin to glow with hot colour. 'I wasn't aware I was asking for anything of an intimate nature,' he said slowly fascinated by her blushing which he had thought was obsolete in this modern day and age. 'I merely wanted to know if there were certain subjects I should avoid.'

'No, there aren't,' she shot back tightly, furious with him and herself. *Any* subject was dangerous with him.

'Good.' His voice was smooth and his eyes were narrowed as he took her arm. 'Let's have a glass of champagne before the dancing begins. No doubt you'll be inundated with requests, and as I'm not quite up to dancing yet I shall have to sit and watch.'

She had noticed he was limping slightly, and now she gave herself a mental kick as she realised she hadn't asked how his leg was. She would have done with anyone else—immediately, she told herself wretchedly—but somehow, with Jared Vincent, the magnetic force of his personality had swamped everything else. She took a deep breath and said quietly, 'I'm sorry, I should have asked how you were feeling now.'

'No, you shouldn't.' He smiled at her, a deliciously sexy smile. 'I want you to see me as a tough guy, not some weakling who couldn't keep his rear end on a horse.'

'Anyone can get thrown,' Henrietta protested quickly, not liking the way his words had made her feel. He must know that it was somehow subtly seductive for him to reveal his chagrin—not that she trusted it was genuine for a moment, she told herself firmly. He wasn't the type to be embarrassed about anything, not Jared Vincent.

'I don't.' It was very definite. 'But there's always a first time for everything and that was mine. And the leg's fine, really,' he added softly. 'Getting better every day.'

'Good.' She was blushing again and she really didn't know why but it made her cross. 'I'm glad.'

'Mmm.' He slanted a bright blue look at her from under half-closed lids as he led her through an open doorway and into what appeared to be a beautiful ballroom. 'I wish I could believe that but I think you are only being polite, Henrietta Noake. Still, patience has its own reward,' he finished silkily.

Henrietta opened her mouth to make a tart retort, and then shut it again as she looked up—and up—into the hard dark face above her. He was too clever by half, and she wasn't going to win in a war of words with this big, aggressively attractive man so it was wiser not to try.

Once seated on one of the small, velvet-upholstered straight-backed chairs that lined the ballroom, a uniformed waiter was immediately at their side with a tray of sparkling glasses filled with champagne. Jared thanked him and took two, passing Henrietta hers with another piercing glance as he said, 'Do you enjoy dancing, Henrietta?'

'Sometimes.' She shrugged carefully, allowing her eyelashes to shade her eyes as she took a sip of the deliciously effervescent wine. At one time—in pre-Melvyn days—she had adored dancing, along with parties and nightclubs and everything connected with fun and laughter and youth, but within weeks of her marriage such places had become minefields where her merest glance, the slightest smile at a member of the opposite sex, had provoked such blazing explosions of rage that she had become conditioned to robot formality. And since Melvyn's death almost thirteen months ago, when they had been married just a year, she had felt she would never want to smile or dance or be merry again.

It had made her sad when she'd thought about it, that her husband had taken that part of her—the confident, easy-going, insouciant part of her—down with him to the grave, but once she had taken up residence at the mill and begun to take control of her life again it hadn't bothered her so much. She had acquired Murphy two weeks before moving to Herefordshire—from an animal rehoming service where he had been placed because the family who had bought him as a puppy hadn't allowed for him growing into such an enormous animal—and with her need to support them both and her absorption and pleasure in her work, along with Murphy's unconditional love and loyalty, she had gradually clawed back some measure of peace of mind in the isolated surroundings.

Jared sat down beside her, his eyes still intent as he said, 'Only sometimes? I would have put you down as a natural dancer. You have a grace, an elegance and poise about you that would lend itself well to rhythm and movement.'

Henrietta stared at him suspiciously. Part of Melvyn's strategy for domination and control had been to tell her she was clumsy and stupid, and after a time she had begun to believe it in spite of herself. Since her marriage she had found it difficult to accept compliments, and that legacy—along with the guilt and pain and general self-abasement that she now had to fight against every day of her life—made her voice wary as she said, 'Thank you, but I don't think I'm graceful.'

'Ah, but we never see ourselves as others see us, Henrietta.' And now the blue gaze was like a laser beam boring straight into her mind. 'Some people are blessed by the sort of self-assurance that makes them fearless and confident at best, and egotistical and overbearing at worst, and others are insecure and painfully vulnerable whatever their natural attributes. It's all down to the shaping of an individual by life's circumstances and, of course, their genetic make-up.'

She didn't like the way their conversation was going; it was too deep and much too intrusive. He was too perceptive by half, she acknowledged nervously, and once he got the faint notion of something he was like a dog with a bone.

'You don't agree?' He had registered her withdrawal, her body language tense as she gripped the champagne flute until her knuckles gleamed white, and now his voice was soft and even.

'I suppose so.' She shrugged jerkily, her voice tight in spite of her effort to sound unconcerned. 'I've never thought about it.'

Maybe. And maybe not. One thing was for sure—what you saw was most definitely not what you got with Henrietta Noake, Jared thought as he took a huge swallow of his own champagne, half emptying the glass. And here he was, stuck in a corner like some lame beggar at the feast. No doubt half the men here would want to dance with her, and the other half would only be prevented from doing so by the wrath of jealous wives. She looked beautiful tonight, but there was something more than good looks, something…elusive. It would draw the men like a magnet.

He was right—it did. Once the dancing got underway Henrietta found there was no shortage of partners, but wherever she was in the massive ballroom, and whoever she was with, she was burningly conscious of a big dark figure at one side of the room. She knew the moment anyone stopped to talk to him, and she noted—with a little ache in her heart region she despised herself for—that there was a constant stream of women about him, laughing, chatting, or simply looking adoringly up into his face.

He was nothing more than a philanderer, she told herself with a touch of bitterness as she glanced over the shoulder of her present dance partner to see the willowy blonde he had been talking to when she had first seen him that evening kiss him full on the mouth before she rose from her seat at his side. No doubt he was a playboy at heart; he certainly had the wealth and connections to indulge himself wherever his fancy took him.

But it was no concern of hers what he did, she reminded herself in the next instant. He was a free agent when all was said and done, and answerable to no one.

She found she was frowning as her partner whirled her round the floor and quickly forced her face into more amenable lines as she caught his rather surprised glance. Pull yourself together, she told herself sharply, and at least *act* as though you are having a good time.

'Henrietta?'

'What?' She blinked up into the enquiring, middle-aged face as she realised he had been talking and she hadn't heard a word. 'I'm sorry,' she apologised quickly, 'I didn't quite catch that.'

'I asked you if you feel nervous at all at the mill,' Ronald Glenfield—Jared's estate manager—repeated patiently.

'Oh, no, not with Murphy,' Henrietta said immediately. 'He's—'

'The Hound of the Baskervilles?' Ronald supplied with a wry grin. 'Jared's already told me about your German shepherd.'

'Is that what he calls Murphy?' Too late Ronald realised Henrietta was deeply offended. 'Murphy is as gentle as a lamb,' she said steadily, 'and he wouldn't hurt a fly except to protect me. You ought to see him with my brother's children; they absolutely adore him. And Jared's got no right to call him that; he was perfectly behaved that night when Jared turned up on our doorstep.'

'Granted.' The deep dark voice behind her could only belong to one man, and as Jared touched Ronald's arm and said, 'I'm stealing Henrietta for a few minutes, okay?' Henrietta swung round to see him just behind her.

'And I love your dog.' The grave apology followed before she could speak. 'Truly, I do. And he was a model of decorum, nothing less.

In fact for sheer good manners and propriety Murphy is a prince in the canine world.'

Henrietta tried, she really tried, to be angry, but there was something about the smiling blue eyes in the serious male face that made her want to giggle.

'And I'm very pleased the word has got about that he's with you in that lonely mill,' Jared added softly, suddenly deadly serious, 'but as an added precaution I'm having an alarm fitted after Christmas.'

'What?' Henrietta couldn't have been more taken aback.

'It'll be linked up with the local police station,' Jared continued imperturbably, 'although just the sight of a flashing light with some noise would be enough to scare away the sort of itinerant opportunist that might look on the mill as a nice place to spend the night. And once they caught sight of Murphy's fangs...'

'An alarm isn't necessary,' she protested sharply, her voice high-pitched. 'I've been there since February and I've been perfectly all right. In fact you are the only unannounced visitor we've had,' she added meaningfully.

'Nevertheless, it's something I've been thinking of doing for some time,' Jared lied sincerely. 'I spent a considerable amount of money on that old mill; look on it as a protection of my investment. What with squatter's rights these days, and court orders and such, prevention is better than the long-drawn-out and often acrimonious cure.'

'I suppose so.' Henrietta considered the matter, her head tilted to one side. Friar's Mill was a beautifully and sensitively restored property and she could understand Jared wanting to protect it from wandering vagabonds and the like. Murphy was more than enough of a deterrent in the normal run of things, but if they were away for a few days or something of that nature... And she *did* have that special exhibition of her work due in April. Her mother had already made it clear that she would expect her daughter to be in London at that time. 'Yes, I can see you want to protect your property,' she said after a few moments. 'I think I'd do the same if the mill were mine.'

'That's settled, then.' Considering the idea had only occurred to him as he had watched her glide round the room with a variety of captivated partners, Jared felt immensely relieved. 'Now, come and have something to eat,' he said smoothly as he drew her towards the open doorway into the hall. 'You can dance some more later.'

But she didn't want to dance if she could be with him instead. The sudden knowledge was terrifying, and caused her to miss her step and stumble as they left the ballroom behind them.

'Careful.' His hand was at her elbow, his touch firm and arrogantly sure as he drew her into his side. 'I'm the one with the gammy leg, remember?' he said lightly.

She tried to return his easy smile but it was beyond her. This was dangerous—*he* was dangerous—and she had known it all along. What was she doing? she asked herself feverishly. Was she one of those women who was drawn to the wrong type of man time and time again in spite of all the warning signs?

Before Melvyn—in the days when she had been young and sure of herself—she had been utterly bewildered by some women's naiveté in the love stakes. *She* would never allow any man to tyrannise her, she had told herself with the confidence of youth. A relationship had to be built on equal terms for it to survive; any less and all the signs of decay were there.

But it wasn't as simple as that. She knew that now. And that bold, dauntless girl of yesteryear was nothing but a faint memory.

The hot and cold buffet was amazing, and already folk were tucking in as though there was no tomorrow, but Henrietta found she had no appetite as Jared escorted her from dish to dish. She should never have come here tonight, she told herself frantically as people made way for them as though Jared was the king and she his consort. It was madness, *madness*.

As though to contest the thought, Jared's voice was the epitome of gentleness as he said, 'You haven't taken enough to feed a bird. Let me get you some more.'

'No, no, I'm fine. I'm just not hungry tonight, that's all,' Henrietta said brightly, her stomach churning. Melvyn had been gentle at the beginning, so gentle, she remembered darkly. In fact he hadn't been able to do enough for her; her slightest wish had been his command. And that side of him had never completely gone away— that was the very thing that had been so difficult to understand. If he had been *all* bad her course of action would have been so much clearer and he might even be alive this very day. As it was his life had been cut short at the painfully young age of twenty-seven, and the world had lost a brilliant sculptor...

'Hey, nothing can be as bad as that.'

Henrietta came out of the black void her thoughts had taken her into to find Jared peering down at her, his piercing eyes trained on hers.

'I'm sorry.' She forced a quick smile and prayed he would let the matter drop. It was a vain prayer.

'What is it, Henrietta?' He had steered her into a quiet corner of the huge dining room and now he took her plate from her, placing it on a chair along with his own before straightening and facing her. 'And don't tell me nothing,' he added softly as she opened her mouth to say that very thing, 'because it won't wash. Are you in trouble of some kind?'

'No, Jared, I'm not in any trouble,' Henrietta said steadily, but when she would have dropped her chin he raised it with a gentle finger so she was forced to look into his dark face.

'What is it, then? What was making you look like that just now?' he persisted tenaciously, his mouth set in a stubborn line that told her prevarication would be useless. He had no *right* to question her like this Henrietta told herself helplessly, but then she already knew that Jared Vincent was a law unto himself. Well, she would tell him so much and no more, and maybe it would convince him further interest in her was useless? He was the sort of man who indulged in light flirtations, that was crystal-clear, and if the number of women who had been hovering round him tonight were anything to go by he wouldn't have to look far for his next affair.

'I was just thinking.' She paused, and then forced herself to go on, but it was difficult. This was the first time she had mentioned Melvyn to anyone but family and close friends since his death. 'About my husband,' she continued quietly.

'Your *what*?' It didn't sound like Jared's voice at all.

She hadn't meant it to sound quite so stark but now, as she stared into his incredulous face, she saw he had misconstrued her words. For a moment she was tempted to let him think that her husband *was* still around, but she couldn't, and so she added, 'My late husband,' and saw the dawning knowledge in his appalled eyes.

'You're a widow?' he asked unsteadily. 'At your age?'

If the situation had been different there would have been something funny about his total amazement—Henrietta doubted if much surprised Jared Vincent—but, as it was, amusement was the furthest thing from her mind when she said, her voice low, 'Yes, I'm a widow. My...husband died just over a year ago. We had been married thirteen months.'

'I think I need to sit down.' He pulled her down beside him and there was absolute silence for a moment or two before he said, 'What was it? An accident of some kind? He must have been young…?'

'He was twenty-seven.' She paused, and then centred her gaze on a particular pattern in the magnificent Persian carpet at their feet. 'And yes, Melvyn was killed in a car accident, although not the normal kind. We…were walking along the pavement and a stolen car driven by a fifteen-year-old boy went out of control. Melvyn pushed me out of the way but there wasn't time to save himself,' she finished flatly. 'He died instantly.'

'Henrietta, I don't know what to say.' She felt Jared's hand gently touch her cheek, but she didn't raise her eyes and after a moment his touch was gone. 'I had no idea; you sign yourself as Miss Noake,' he said softly.

'I…I reverted to my maiden name after the funeral,' Henrietta said awkwardly. She was feeling awful, terrible, about his obviously genuine horror and sympathy, but she'd started this now and there was no going back. 'So that's why I…I don't date,' she said quietly. 'And I prefer my own company, mine and Murphy's.'

'Yes, I see.' There was another silence, longer this time, and then he said, 'You must have loved him very much, Henrietta, and I'm sorry I forced you to speak of it when it's clearly still so hard for you.' His voice was soft and very controlled.

'No, it's all right.' His tenderness was heaping coals of fire on her head and her cheeks were burning with the heat of them.

'It's not all right,' he countered evenly. 'I rarely make assumptions about people—I learnt the hard way when I was much younger that it's potentially dangerous—but I did about you. I apologise.'

She would remember this if she was ever tempted to try a bit of manipulation again, Henrietta thought bleakly. She clearly didn't have what it took. From what she had told him, Jared had assumed she was still in love with Melvyn, and that was what she had wanted him to believe a few minutes ago. Now, *now* she wasn't so sure. Suddenly it felt wrong, deceitful, to leave it like this. But she couldn't explain fully; she just couldn't. She didn't understand it all herself, even the way she felt, so how could she possibly unload the whole mess on someone else?

She raised a pale, bleak face from which all guilty colour had fled, leaving it deathly white, to Jared's watching eyes, and saw a totally different man from the sensual, slightly wicked, mocking philanderer she was used to. And it didn't help. It didn't help at all. There was a reserve in his eyes now, a definite withdrawal, and, ridiculous though it was, she felt the loss in every bone of her body as his warm, sympathetic and terribly attractive face looked back at her.

And she didn't feel any better as the evening progressed. She danced when she was asked, she smiled and chatted, but she couldn't rid herself of the faint ache of regret that had been with her since her revelation. He would leave her alone now and that was what she had wanted, wasn't it? she told herself fiercely as another partner deposited her back to Jared's side with a laughing compliment.

And as he talked to her in the few minutes before another dance was claimed she had the feeling she had been relegated to maiden aunt status in that intelligent, sharp and surprisingly sensitive brain, and perversely it was incredibly galling.

It was much later in the evening, as the first guests began to leave, that Jared bent down to her and said, his voice quiet, 'Are you going back to London for the Christmas holiday, Henrietta? I presume your family would like to see you?'

'I thought about it.'

She paused, intending to explain that her mother's beautiful apartment with its cream carpets and pale lemon furnishings was not conducive to a harmonious Christmas with Murphy in residence, but before she could go on Jared cut in with, 'But it would revive too many painful memories? Yes, I understand.'

No, you don't understand. Henrietta stared at him, a mixture of frustration and irritation clouding her eyes. Why did he have to be so darn nice about all this? she asked herself, with an immediate feeling of guilt at her unreasonableness.

'No, it's not that,' she said quickly. 'It's just that Murphy and I will be more comfortable at the mill. He's a big dog, and my mother doesn't really care for animals.'

'I see.' It was clear he didn't believe her, his lean dark face sombre. 'Then perhaps you would do me the honour of dining at Fotheringham on Christmas Day?' he asked formally.

Good grief, he was even *talking* as though she had aged a few decades, Henrietta thought testily, before she forced down the exasperation—which was all her own fault, no one else's, she reminded herself silently—and said, 'Thank you, but we'll be fine.' Pity she could do without. 'I've promised Murphy a nice long walk and then a late dinner of turkey and roast potatoes by the fire.'

'Sounds wonderful.' And suddenly a touch of the old Jared was back as he grinned and added, 'If it wasn't for the fact that we're going to be deluged with relations from all parts of the globe, I'd angle for an invitation myself.'

And then Henrietta went hot as he bent his big body and put his face so close that she could smell the warm male scent of him and feel the rough texture of his chin as he whispered in her ear, 'I loathe Christmas at Fotheringham but I'm locked into a tradition that goes way back.'

'It doesn't mean you have to continue it indefinitely, does it?' she whispered back, her stomach knotting at the expensively sensual aftershave he was wearing.

'No, I guess not.' He straightened, staring down at her for a moment before he admitted wryly, 'I suppose if I'm being truthful I've never cared enough to change it; there's never been anything better on offer. Parties, dinner, cocktails... They're the same at Fotheringham as anywhere else.' He shrugged massive shoulders, his flagrant masculinity more pronounced than ever as he surveyed her through narrowed blue eyes. 'And that's Christmas.'

'When I was younger, much younger—about ten, I think—my parents took David and I up to Scotland one Christmas and we spent a week in a log cabin in the wilds of nowhere,' Henrietta said slowly. She didn't know why the memory had come so sharply into her mind, but now she could almost smell the biting northern air and the heady scent of pine needles from the endlessly tall pines surrounding the cabin. 'David and I had a wonderful time playing in the snow and doing all the things that kids do, and my dad loved every minute—unlike my mother.' She grimaced at the dark face watching her so intently. 'She is a real city dweller; she hated every minute.'

'Where is your father now?' Jared asked softly, sensing she didn't often talk like this and wondering how long he could keep the conversation going before she withdrew into that formidable shell of hers.

'He died when I was sixteen,' Henrietta said softly. 'He was a wonderful man, but my parents were absolute opposites. He liked the great outdoors, my mother has to be forced to even take a walk unless the weather is exactly right. Strange, isn't it? But they were deeply in love until the day he died.'

'So your childhood was a happy one?' His voice was still quiet and steady, but there was something, the merest inflexion, that brought her eyes shooting to the hard male face.

'Yes, very.' And she had often blessed the fact in the black nightmare months of her marriage, knowing that solid base was the only thing that had kept her halfway sane. 'Was yours?' she asked suddenly before she had time to consider her words.

'No; no, it wasn't.' Henrietta stared at him and it was as though a dark mask came over his face, veiling his thoughts and eyes as he said, his voice cool, 'Can I get you another drink, Henrietta?'

It was a definite warning not to probe further and Henrietta was so taken aback it was a full ten seconds before she said, 'Yes, thank you. A soft drink, please—orange or something?'

She watched him as he weaved his way across the dance floor, which was beginning to empty, and it was only then, as the first shock of surprise began to ebb, that she felt angry.

He had cross-examined her from almost their first meeting—in fact his questions had been nothing short of an interrogation at times, she thought furiously—and she asked one thing— just one—and she got the cold shoulder. What a cheek, what a twenty-four-carat cheek. Oh, why hadn't she told him so? she asked herself with the frustration of hindsight. She should have made it perfectly clear he was out of order, but she had just stood there like an idiot. Melvyn had used to browbeat her like that, until she'd hardly been able to say boo to a goose in the end, and she was blowed, she was *blowed* if she would let anyone ever do it again. When he came back she was going to tell him exactly what she thought.

A voice at her elbow interrupted her angry thoughts as Mrs Baker's familiar tones said, 'Ah, there you are, m'dear. Me and Harold are ready to go now, if that's all right with you? Or we can hang on for a bit if you'd rather?'

'No, I'm more than ready,' Henrietta agreed quickly.

'We'll go and get our coats, then, shall we?' The little woman smiled cheerfully. 'We can say our goodbyes to Mr Jared on the way out.'

That suited her just fine. Henrietta's chin was up and her shoulders back as she followed Mrs

Baker's squat rotund shape across the dance floor and into the large cloakroom at the side of it where the guests' coats had been put earlier. A brisk, formal word of thanks in Mr and Mrs Baker's company would finish this somewhat disastrous evening more cleanly than what she'd had in mind a few seconds ago. And this way it would be more dignified at least, she told herself reassuringly. And after what she'd told him, and his changed attitude to her, it was doubtful if their paths would cross again. Which, without any doubt, was the best thing all round.

She was just following the Bakers from the cloakroom to the crowded hall when a deep voice stopped her in her tracks. 'You've changed your mind about that drink?' Jared said evenly just behind her. 'You're leaving?'

'Yes.' She swung round quickly, forcing a bright smile to her face as she said, 'Mrs Baker wants to go; we were just going to say our good-byes to you first.' And then, before he could say anything more, she called, 'Mrs Baker? Mr Vincent is here.'

The Bakers turned and retraced their steps, and for a few minutes Mrs Baker monopolised the conversation with her own brand of gushing appreciation, and Henrietta was more than glad to let her. She just wanted to get home now, home where she could *think*.

'Come along, Ida.'

It was Mr Baker who finished what had become something of an embarrassing situation by the simple expedient of taking his wife's arm and hauling her away, and after a hasty, 'Goodbye, Jared, and thank you very much for a lovely evening,' Henrietta followed without a backward glance.

And that would have been that, Henrietta was to tell herself much later, if the Bakers' car hadn't chosen that particular night, of all nights, to have a flat battery.

Cars were leaving all around them now in a steady flow, and as Henrietta sat in the back of the Bakers' immaculate old Escort listening to Mrs Baker instruct her husband on the advantages of regular car maintenance, during which time his neck got redder and redder, she prayed that the next turn of the ignition would persuade the engine to start. It didn't.

She had glanced back at the house once, just in time to see Jared standing at the top of the large circular steps with the light behind him throwing his big body into silhouette, with a tall, languid blonde draped across his chest. She had turned her head away so quickly that her neck had made a snapping sound.

Whoever that girl was, she didn't mind everyone knowing where her fancy lay, Henrietta thought tightly as she kept her eyes trained strictly in front of her. Not that she cared—of course she didn't—she just didn't like to see any woman make quite such a spectacle of herself, she told herself self-righteously, ignoring the slightly sickly feeling in the pit of her stomach.

She had been close to the blonde once during the dancing and the woman was quite stunningly beautiful, her pale golden hair swept into a sophisticated knot on the top of her head and her flawless skin and huge greeny-grey eyes perfect.

And then, just when Henrietta thought Mr Baker was going to explode at his wife, there was a tap on the driver's window and a cool dark voice said, 'Can I be of any help, Mr Baker?'

Henrietta turned her head with a terrible feeling of inevitability to see Jared standing at the side of the car, his rugged face expressionless and the blonde still firmly attached to his arm like a golden limpet.

This was all she needed, Henrietta told herself silently as the three of them scrambled out of the car into the cold, frosty air. It was as far from the cool, gracious exit she had hoped to make as it was possible to be, especially when Mrs Baker made matters worse by continuing to expound her thoughts as to the cause of their predicament until Mr Baker's patient, placid exterior crumpled and he told his wife, in no uncertain terms, where to put her theories.

Henrietta was painfully conscious of the blonde's aloof, amused face as she surveyed them all as though they were bugs under a microscope, her arm still tucked in Jared's, and when she said, 'Perhaps I might offer some assistance, Jared? I came in the Mercedes tonight,' Henrietta knew she wasn't even going to try to fight the flood of dislike that swamped her.

'Don't worry, Anastasia,' Jared said easily.

Anastasia? Henrietta thought waspily. Well, of course, it had to be, didn't it? Not for this vision of loveliness any ordinary kind of name.

'Mr and Mrs Baker live in the village but Miss Noake is staying at Friar's Mill, and I don't think the Mercedes would appreciate that half a mile of unmade road after the rain and sludge of the last few days. I'll take them home in the Range Rover,' he continued quietly, 'but it was nice of you to offer.'

Jared and the Ice-Queen were discussing them as though they were a delivery of parcels,

Henrietta thought exasperatedly, and she, for
one, didn't appreciate being referred to in the
third person, as though she were too dim-witted
to understand.

'That's really not necessary.' Henrietta drew
herself up and aimed for cool firmness. 'If I may
use the phone and call a taxi? I'm sure we won't
have to wait long.'

'I wouldn't dream of it.' Jared was equally
cool and equally firm. 'The Range Rover is already out.' He indicated an authoritative, gleaming monster of a vehicle standing next to a
crouching sleek red Ferrari. The two vehicles
were parked some distance from the rest of the
cars in a slight incline in the massive forecourt,
and Henrietta just knew they both belonged to
him. 'So it's no trouble,' he added determinedly.

'Oh, but it is.' The bit was between
Henrietta's teeth. 'It's gone one in the morning,
it's cold and frosty, and surely you shouldn't be
driving yet after your accident?'

It was quite the wrong thing to say. The hard
face straightened, the narrowed eyes took on the
consistency of blue ice and his mouth became
grim. 'I'm not a cripple, Henrietta,' he said
evenly, 'and I've been driving again for a full
week now. You'll be quite safe.' The last sen-
tence was referring to more than just his driving

ability, and caused the colour to surge into her cheeks.

She stared at him, and he stared back. 'Thank you.' It was a *fait accompli* and Henrietta knew it. She could hardly object further without causing a scene. 'If you're sure it's no trouble.'

'On the contrary, it's a pleasure,' he said in the sort of tone that belied the content of the words.

'If you're quite sure I can't help, I'd better be on my way, Jared,' Anastasia purred sweetly, her big, heavily lashed eyes flicking over Henrietta once more before they dismissed her as unimportant. 'Don't forget Daddy has invited you for pre-lunch drinks tomorrow before all your guests start arriving in the afternoon.'

'I haven't forgotten, Anastasia, but like I said I'll have to see how things go. Christmas Eve is always something of a bear garden at Fotheringham as you know.'

Jared's voice and his manner were preoccupied, and the beautiful blonde's soft, full mouth tightened for a moment before she laughed lightly, flicking at his broad chest with a red-taloned hand as she said softly, 'Don't worry, darling, I'll come and rescue you now and again. You know you can rely on me.'

I bet he can. Henrietta watched Anastasia reach up and kiss the dark, masculine cheek with something akin to amusement in her eyes. But if it was humour it was of the black kind. The other woman was mad about him, that much was patently obvious, but how did Jared feel? The hard male face was giving nothing away, and neither was his voice as he turned to the three of them, his hand under Anastasia's elbow, and said, 'Will you excuse me for a moment? I'm just seeing Lady Filmore to her car.'

Lady Filmore. Well, well, well.

Jared was back within a minute or two, and now, as the four of them walked over the massive forecourt to the gleaming metallic-blue Range Rover she saw he was limping badly, and her voice was one of genuine concern as she said softly, 'Jared, are you sure you feel okay to drive?'

'I'm fine.' It was something of a snap, and then, as he looked down into her face, his own softened, and he added, 'Really, don't worry. It always aches by this time of night after a long day, that's all. And the Range Rover drives itself.'

They had reached the two vehicles as he spoke, and now, as he helped Mr and Mrs Baker into the leather-clad interior of the Range Rover and then opened the passenger door for Henrietta, she climbed in without saying anything more.

It was her first experience of a four-wheel-drive vehicle, and Henrietta was immediately aware that an ordinary car seemed almost claustrophobic by comparison. The cream leather interior of the cabin with its blue trim was both elegant and comfortable, and the airy spaciousness and abundant headroom and legroom were perfectly suited to Jared's great height. It was unashamedly luxurious, and the 4.6 litre engine growled into immediate life at Jared's touch.

It made her valiant little Mini, which was filled to capacity once she and Murphy were installed, look a little the worse for wear, Henrietta thought wryly as she glanced round the beautiful vehicle; but then, as she became fully aware of Jared at the side of her and the power and authority in the big male figure, she felt something quiver deep inside and directed her gaze at the massive windscreen.

Henrietta found she didn't have to say much at all on the drive to the village—Mrs Baker didn't let anyone else get a word in—but once the other two had been deposited on their doorstep, with Jared promising he would have their car delivered back the next day once his mechanic had seen to it, the atmosphere in the car tightened and stretched.

The night was very dark once they left the lights of the village behind and turned towards the direction of Friar's Mill, the black sky overhead lit only by a thin, crescent moon and myriad twinkling stars, a thick velvet blanket that wrapped the countryside in charcoal-grey shadows.

When the silence became so loud she couldn't bear it, Henrietta forced herself to say, 'It was a lovely party, Jared. I understand you hold one each Christmas for the village and your friends hereabouts?'

'Yes.' The monosyllable was not conducive to further conversation, and by the time they turned off the road and down on to the track which led to Friar's Mill Henrietta had determined she wouldn't try to ease the electric atmosphere again. He was arrogant and difficult and as changeable as the wind, she told herself silently as the powerful vehicle glided disdainfully over the holes and bumps that had shaken her little Mini into a state of collapse. Talk about blowing hot and cold—one minute all over her, then treating her like his grandmother, and now the strong and silent macho man. Well, he might be lord of the manor in this little part of England but as far as she was concerned he was just like any other man. Sort of.

She had left several lights burning in the mill to light the way, and as the Range Rover glided to a regal halt Henrietta prepared herself for a brief word of thanks and a quick getaway, and then Jared took the wind completely out of her sails.

'I'm sorry, Henrietta. Hell, I always seem to be saying that to you, don't I?' he said softly as he cut the engine and silence engulfed them. 'But it's true none the less.'

'You're sorry?' She had turned to look at him once he'd spoken, but he was staring straight ahead, his dark profile barely visible. 'I don't understand,' she said carefully.

'You've been very honest with me tonight, and I appreciate it—' oh, don't, don't turn the knife in the wound, Henrietta thought guiltily, glad of the darkness to hide her red face '—but when you asked me about my childhood... Well, it's a subject I don't talk about,' he said expressionlessly.

'Oh, I see.' She was stiff and tense, and just didn't know what to say next.

'I have a lot of bad memories about my childhood and teenage years,' Jared continued, a trace of bitterness evident for the first time, 'which is one of the reasons I prefer to limit my time at Fotheringham to the bare minimum. I only came back when I did in November because the project I'd been working on in America for the last nine months was finished, and with Christmas on the horizon and the traditions that go with it it seemed simpler to come home earlier than normal. However, that didn't work out quite as planned.' He turned to look at her then, a wry smile on his face as he gestured at his leg.

'No.' She nodded her agreement, but in view of what had gone before felt unable to ask him anything and began to fumble in her bag for her key. 'I'd better go in; Murphy will be wondering—'

'You're very sweet, do you know that?' His voice was husky now and the darkness was warm and consuming within the air-conditioned vehicle as he smiled his magnetic smile, his hard face mellowing and his eyes crinkling at the corners.

She had to stop this. She knew what he wanted—the knowledge was quivering between them like a live thing and causing her heart to race and the blood to pound in her ears—and it mustn't happen. She couldn't get involved with anyone—be it a brief affair or whatever—and certainly, *certainly* not Jared Vincent. He would eat her up and spit her out without even noticing.

But even as she thought it he leant over towards her, his voice thick as he murmured her name.

She actually trembled as she felt the touch of his lips stroke hers, and with his nearness the warm, sensual scent of him was all about her and it was intoxicating. And he knew how to kiss. She was aware of that in the next moment too. This wasn't a wet, clumsy assault on her senses, but a sweet, delicate fuelling of pleasure as he allowed the kiss to deepen moment by moment until little frissons of desire were shivering up and down her spine.

And he didn't rush her. Even as he pulled her closer to him, his hand moving to the small of her back as he positioned her more to his liking, he was feeding her pleasure as carefully as his own.

But Melvyn had known how to kiss too, and he had been dangerously gentle and persuasive and thrilling at the beginning.

The thought came from nowhere, but it had the power to catapult her back in her seat and against the side of the door panel with a force that caused Jared to growl, 'What the...?'

'I'm sorry, I am, but I don't want this.' She wrenched at the door handle and almost tumbled out into the open, just managing to keep on her feet when she landed on the rough gravel.

'Henrietta, for crying out loud, listen to me.' He had followed her out of the Range Rover and now, as he reached her side, he said, 'I'm not going to hurt you or make you do anything you don't want to do. It was just a goodnight kiss.'

'I don't want goodnight kisses, don't you see?' she said breathlessly, utterly panic-stricken. 'I just want to be left alone, that's all. I *came* to the mill to be left alone.'

'All right, all right.' Jared held up soothing hands as he stepped back a pace. 'I get the message.'

'I mean it.' It wasn't Jared Vincent in front of her but a tall, dashingly handsome man with long hair and dancing eyes—eyes that could turn into razor-sharp weapons that had the power to terrify her in a moment of time. Melvyn had been mercurial, a volatile, brilliant and frighteningly unstable genius whose capriciousness had had a dark power which captivated and bewitched.

And the last thing she wanted was to get close to anyone again, even a kiss close. If she kept her defences up and her eyes wide open she wouldn't get hurt again. It really was as simple as that.

'I know you mean it, Henrietta.' Jared's face was expressionless now, and cold, very cold.

'I like my life just the way it is,' Henrietta said jerkily as she backed towards the heavy old oak door of the mill. 'I have my work and Murphy for company, and that suits me just fine. Thank you for tonight,' she added as her frantic fingers found her key and she turned and opened the door. 'Goodnight.'

She didn't know whether he replied or not— she had already fallen into the tiny square flag-stoned hall and shut the door behind her—but as she leant against the aged wood, Murphy leaping about her in an ecstasy of greeting, her heart was pounding so hard she thought it would burst.

There was what seemed a million years of silence outside before she heard the engine that signalled his departure, and she was still leaning against the door some long minutes later—with Murphy now sitting in front of her, head cocked to one side as he considered the point of this new game—as she willed her heartbeat to return to normal.

Jared must think she was stark staring mad. Henrietta gazed down into Murphy's puzzled brown eyes as humiliation washed over her in great black waves. How *could* she have reacted like that to a simple goodnight kiss? She wrapped her arms round her waist, hugging herself in an agony of embarrassment.

But that was it—it hadn't been simple, not for her at any rate. She had enjoyed it. Not only enjoyed it, *relished* it, she admitted in silent remorse.

'Oh, Murphy...' It was a painful groan, and now the big German shepherd pricked up his ears before whining in commiseration deep in his throat. 'How could I have been so stupid? I shouldn't have let him kiss me, and when he did I could have handled it better than that, couldn't I? I've been married, for goodness' sake, and he knows that, and yet I acted like some outraged virgin fighting for her virtue.'

Murphy's deep sigh told her he understood her misery but was powerless to help.

'Well, that's it.' She stared down into the devoted eyes and nodded her head in mortification. 'He'll think I'm completely round the bend and avoid this place like the plague.' And as she wanted nothing more to do with him that was all for the best, wasn't it? Her thoughts were racing but this last one did nothing to soothe her anguish.

'I hate men, Murphy.' It was bleak and desolate and didn't ring true even to her own ears, and she was only arguing with herself when she reiterated more strongly, 'I do, I hate them all,' before marching through to the kitchen and settling Murphy in his basket for the night with a big, bone-shaped biscuit.

CHAPTER FOUR

IT PROVED to be a mild New Year, and spring came early at the mill with warm sunny days full of blossom and primroses and drifts of delicate snowdrops.

In April the river was full of life, tiny freshwater shrimps, coddis fly larvae, little fish and endless insects bringing a host of birds to its shores every day, all of which proved a wonderful backdrop to Henrietta's paintings.

Her studio was situated in an annexe attached to the mill which had been stables at one time, before Jared had had the mill restored from its derelict state and converted into a beautiful home. The annexe was basically a huge rectangular room with its own small cloakroom holding a washbasin and toilet at the far end, and had been planned to double as a study, an extra lounge area, even a small guest suite—in fact whatever the occupier desired of it.

The massive windows which ran down all of one wall and looked out on to open countryside made it the perfect place to paint, and when Henrietta had first seen the property and mentioned her desire to use the annexe as a pottery studio—along with her painting—it had been agreed on the understanding she would restore the room to its former state when, and if, she left when the three-year lease was up.

So, the carpet had been rolled up and taken away by Jared's agent a few days before Henrietta had arranged for the kiln, clay bins, electric wheel, concrete slab and all the numerous other pieces of equipment connected with a home studio to be delivered. There was already an extractor fan close to where Henrietta had planned to house the kiln, and once her tools and equipment were in place it had seemed as though the annexe had been purpose-built for her needs.

She was very, very lucky. Henrietta told herself this on a fresh April morning as she stood looking out of the huge windows at the rolling countryside stretching away from her, bleating sheep in the fields beyond looking like white dots on the landscape, and a soaring buzzard in the cloudless blue sky above sweeping and diving in its search for prey.

There was a profusion of wild flowers now in the lanes and field surrounding the mill, and she often felt like an Edwardian lady as she tramped the countryside with Murphy at her side and her paints and easel under her arm.

Yes, she was lucky. She nodded sharply at the thought. And she wasn't a bit concerned that Jared Vincent hadn't been near the mill since Christmas. Not a bit. *She wasn't.*

She turned and glanced at the suitcase and holdall standing by the studio door. All her pots and paintings had gone up to London the week before, courtesy of her brother's great transit van, and now the only other thing needed at the exhibition of her work—commencing the next day—was her presence.

Much to her mother's chagrin she had declined the offer of her spare room—the proposal hadn't included Murphy, and Henrietta hadn't felt inclined to put him in kennels for four days while she languished in luxury in her mother's cream and pastel-coloured apartment—and had instead leapt at the suggestion of her brother's tiny boxroom. It would be a tight fit for her and Murphy but her brother's family adored the huge German shepherd, and Sarah—David's wife—and the children would be company for the dog while she was out all day at the exhibition.

'Come on, Murphy, time to make a move.' He was at her feet—where he had been all morning since he had observed her packing, as though his presence underfoot emphasised she mustn't even think of leaving him behind—and now she stroked the velvet ears before the two of them walked through into the ground floor of the mill after Henrietta had collected her suitcase and holdall.

The drive to London was uneventful, and after calling in at the gallery and having a word with her mother and David—Murphy waiting in the Mini as patiently as though butter wouldn't melt in his mouth—she drove to David's home. There Murphy received a deliriously rapturous greeting from her three small nieces and nephew, and they all ate chilli and baked potatoes—Murphy included—once David got home.

The next day Henrietta didn't feel quite so relaxed. In fact she was as taut as piano wire at the daunting thought of the impending exhibition when she climbed into David's smart new Jaguar after breakfast, her brother having insisted she ride into town with him. 'You can't possibly draw up outside the gallery in that heap on wheels,' David had said disparagingly with a scathing glance at the battered Mini. 'What if someone *sees* you?'

Henrietta really couldn't have cared less, but David was her brother and she loved him, and a ride in the Jaguar was a small price to pay to keep him happy. Besides which, reliable though the Mini normally was, there was always a slight element of Russian roulette as to whether she would arrive at her destination on time when she entrusted herself to the decrepit old vehicle.

'You look fabulous.' David had parked at the back of the gallery in the tiny two-car car park, and now, just as they prepared to enter by the side door, he caught hold of Henrietta's hand and squeezed it reassuringly. 'You'll knock 'em dead, sis.'

'It's my work that's on show, not me,' Henrietta answered smilingly, her words belying the two hours she had taken that morning to get ready, discarding two of the outfits she had brought with her before she'd decided on the jade-green dress and knee-length matching jacket she was wearing, which was teamed with high-heeled, ankle-strap shoes of exactly the same shade. Long gold hoops in her ears, and a casual but elegant chignon for her hair with some becoming wisps about her face, and she looked every inch the young, successful woman about town. And that was important if she was ever to build up a regular clientele for her work.

At the moment she was barely scraping by each month, and if it weren't for the nest egg

she had left after Melvyn's affairs were settled—which was steadily dwindling as time
went on—she wouldn't have been able to manage. But the odd opening into one or two of the
more select shops and galleries round about, and
she knew she would be well and truly in the
black. And both her paintings and her pottery
sold well when given the opportunity; it was
getting the viewing space that was the problem.

This first-day viewing was by invitation
only—the next three days would be open to the
general public—and soon after eleven, when the
gallery opened, the first guests began to trickle
in. By lunchtime, when the wine and nibbles
were disappearing fast, David—ever cautious—
whispered in her ear that he thought it was going
surprisingly well, and the little glow his words
induced carried her over the moment, some five
minutes later, when a dark voice just behind her
said, 'That hermit-type existence pays off if
your work is anything to go by.'

'Jared?' She whirled around, her mouth agape
and her heart feeling as though it was trying to
jump out of her chest cavity.

'Hello, Henrietta.' The hard, aggressively attractive face was just as she had pictured it more
times than she would like to remember over the
last four months, and the jet-black hair was

longer, heightening the connection with Melvyn. And yet he wasn't really at all like her dead husband to look at, Henrietta thought fleetingly as she struggled to respond to Jared's cool, controlled greeting. Melvyn had had film-star, classically handsome good looks, and Jared's rugged countenance was anything but that. But the two men *were* similar, under the skin…

She realised she was still gaping at him and quickly smoothed her face into a smile as she said, her voice only shaking the tiniest bit, 'What on earth are you doing here? Did…have you got an invitation?'

'Do I look the sort of man who would gate-crash?'

Actually he did, and her face must have revealed her thoughts because he laughed out loud, shaking his head slightly as he said, 'Henrietta Noake, you'll be the death of me. Yes, my suspicious siren, I do have an invitation,' he confirmed reproachfully.

'How…?' She paused, and then changed her tack as she said, her voice prim, 'I wouldn't have put you down as someone who would be interested in this sort of event.'

'I'm not,' he agreed gravely. 'I'm interested in the artist, and that's quite different, isn't it?'

Henrietta floundered. How on earth could she follow that? And what did he mean he was interested in the artist when she hadn't seen hide nor hair of him since that embarrassing, oh, so terribly embarrassing night before Christmas Eve?

As though in answer to her unvoiced thoughts he continued, 'I had to fly out to the States just after Christmas. A deal I thought was all sewn up and ironed out turned bad, and the resulting fracas was messy.'

'And it took you three months and two weeks to sort it out?' Hell, she hadn't meant to say that, Henrietta thought furiously as she watched the piercing blue eyes widen for one split second before they narrowed in thoughtful contemplation on her hot face.

'Have you been counting the days?' he drawled softly with maddening satisfaction as the black eyebrows rose consideringly.

'No, I have not,' she shot back immediately, every hair bristling. 'I just like people to mean what they say, that's all. And how did you know about my exhibition anyway?'

'Ronald mentioned it.' Jared's tone was elaborately casual now. 'There's nothing wrong with that, is there? It wasn't a secret?'

'No, of course it wasn't a secret.' She eyed him warily. Ronald called by at least once a week now on his rounds about the vast estate since he had supervised the fitting of the burglar alarm at the beginning of the year, and as he was the only person she ever saw—and as he was very happily married with three teenage children and a gorgeous wife—she often invited him in for a piece of home-made fruit cake and a cup of coffee.

Their chats were very light and easy—and she had purposely avoided any mention of Jared— but she had probably mentioned the exhibition although she couldn't remember doing so.

'I indicated to Ronald I'd be in this neck of the woods on business most of this week, and so he kindly arranged for an invitation.' Jared's voice was the epitome of open innocence. 'Nothing devious, perfectly straightforward, see?'

She didn't see anything where this man was concerned, Henrietta thought defensively. She'd had the unworthy feeling just once or twice— which she had immediately dismissed as outrageous and vain—that Ronald's sudden friendship might have something to do with orders from Jared to keep his eye on her, but when the weeks had gone by and Jared had shown no signs of renewing their tenuous acquaintance she had dismissed her suspicions as galloping paranoia. But now...? She gazed into the rivetingly blue eyes and decided she didn't feel strong enough to follow that particular line of enquiry at the moment.

He was here and that was that. All she could do now was to carry this off as best she could, and hope he would have the decency to leave fairly soon.

He didn't.

Henrietta's mother joined them after lunch when her afternoon assistant had arrived to take charge of the shop, and when David—who had been delighted to hear that Jared Vincent was none other than Henrietta's enormously wealthy landlord—introduced her to him Sandra Noake's lovely hazel eyes lit up with speculation.

Henrietta saw the look that passed over her mother's face and inwardly groaned. Her mother was a businesswoman first and foremost, with a ruthless streak that had used to amuse her mild-mannered father, and Jared Vincent was now the quarry. Her mother would sweet-talk him into spending hundreds if he wasn't careful.

The exhibition was due to close its doors at four o'clock, and at half past three Sandra hadn't moved from Jared's side. Within moments of meeting him her mother had steered him into a quiet corner where a couple of comfy easy chairs were tucked in front of a long, low coffee table, and Henrietta had seen a plateful of food followed by a bottle of the very best wine her mother usually kept for only the most élite patrons appear like magic in front of them.

And then they had talked—and talked—and talked. Every time Henrietta glanced across at the dark and fair heads so close together she had inwardly trembled. What was her mother telling him? And what was he asking? They certainly couldn't have kept up a conversation dealing purely with the merits of her work for this length of time, although every time she had made it her business to join them it would appear so. She knew he wasn't genuinely interested in her work—he'd more or less said so, hadn't he, when he'd first arrived? she told herself firmly—and she didn't trust him an inch.

'Darling, he's just gorgeous.' At a quarter to four Sandra had left Jared's side long enough to find Henrietta and whisper conspiratorially in her ear. 'Why on earth haven't you mentioned him before? Because he's clearly mad about you.'

'Of course he isn't.' Henrietta glared at her mother as though she had just received a major insult. 'And I barely know him, that's why I haven't mentioned him,' she said firmly.

'Humph!' Sandra Noake was very good at meaningful exclamations, and now she raised her pencil-thin eyebrows as she said, 'He's bought the four ''Season'' paintings, you know.'

'Has he?' Henrietta didn't know how she felt about that. She had been hoping someone would buy the four paintings and keep them together, but in view of the asking price for each one she had doubted it. But they were, in her opinion, by far the best work she had done in ages. The four, beautifully framed water-colours depicted the changing seasons in all their different but exquisitely delicate beauty, with the old mill as the feature in each with the backdrop of the winding river and fields beyond. 'Well, as Jared owns Friar's Mill no doubt he is looking on them as some sort of investment,' she said weakly.

'No doubt.' Her mother's voice was dry, but she had the good taste not to press further, and her face was gentle as she added, 'Perhaps you ought to say goodbye to him, Hen? It *was* nice of him to come.'

Yes, it was. Henrietta nodded, before taking a deep breath and walking over to where Jared was now standing in front of the paintings he had purchased.

'I particularly like the winter one.' He hadn't glanced at her as she had joined him, but was obviously aware of her presence nevertheless. 'The sky is wonderful. That white light in the silver sky is quite magnificent.'

'Thank you.' Winter was her favourite too, and for the reason he had just imparted, but she wasn't going to tell him that. 'But I hope my mother didn't badger you to buy something. She can be dreadfully tenacious when she gets the bit between her teeth and she doesn't know when to take no for an answer. You mustn't—'

'Henrietta, I love them.' He interrupted her anxious voice with smooth authority as he turned his head to glance down at her. 'And despite what you obviously think of me I do have just the merest modicum of sensitivity that allows me to appreciate art in all its varied forms,' he said drily.

He was doing it again—putting her completely in the wrong, Henrietta thought resentfully.

'And some of your pottery work is quite exceptional.' He drew her with him across the room as he spoke, and short of jerking her arm away from his hand—which in view of the 'Season' sale was out of the question—she could do nothing but go with him. 'This pierced bowl for instance.' He stopped in front of another of her favourites, a plain white but beautifully worked porcelain bowl with the pierced design representing a ring of trees. 'How did you get this effect?'

She glanced up into the hard dark face, wondering if he was just being polite. But there was a look of real interest in the blue eyes as they examined the piece, and suddenly she found herself talking quite naturally. 'The pattern can be pierced through the walls of the pot once the clay is leather-hard,' she explained quietly, 'but it's a fine art as the clay has to be dry enough to withstand pressure applied by the piercing tool without warping, but still be sufficiently plastic not to split. Of course a pattern that involves extensive piercing, like this one, does weaken the structure of the pot.'

'And this one?'

Jared pointed to a large round dish, the inside of which was a swirl of red and gold.

'Ah, now that's an effect we call marbling. Similar to this one—' Henrietta pointed to another dish '—which has been combed, but you can see how it differs…' She moved from piece to piece with Jared at her side as she became immersed in explaining her craft, and then, after some minutes, she surprised a smile on his face as she glanced up suddenly.

'What's the matter?' She was immediately on the defensive, her own face losing its animation and becoming wary as she sensed ridicule. Melvyn had been a master at making her feel foolish.

'Nothing.' He was quick to reassure her. 'It's just that you are so fierce about your work…impassioned. It surprises me you can bear to sell any of it,' he said softly.

Her serious brown eyes surveyed him for a long moment, when he found himself holding his breath, and then she smiled, her face relaxing as she admitted, 'It's very hard. They become a part of me, like children, and there are one or two I've never been able to bring myself to sell.' There had been more than one or two in the past, but in Melvyn's last orgy of jealousy—on the night he had died—he had smashed most of her treasures before she could escape from their apartment, even going so far as to slash her favourite painting—done from an old photograph of her father—into ribbons.

She hadn't realised it until some weeks into their marriage, but he had been resentful and mistrustful of her own creativity, as though he felt it would lessen his hold over her in some way. It wasn't that he'd coveted her gift—his own brilliance had surpassed hers like an eagle soaring above a common garden starling—but he'd wanted to be at the forefront of her mind every minute, every second, with nothing getting in the way.

And then, as she realised Jared was staring at her with a strange expression on his face, she quickly wiped the dark memories away and said with brittle brightness, 'But needs must of course. I've a living to earn.'

'Well, if all this is anything to go by, buyers will soon be beating a path to your door.'

'I doubt that.' Her voice was restrained now, and Jared felt frustration slash at his vitals. So close, and no further. She might as well have said it out loud, he thought grimly. Why was he bothering anyway? She wasn't at all the type he usually went for, with her nervous, wide-eyed way of looking at him as though he were the devil incarnate, and her touch-me-not mentality. She was still in love with this dead husband of hers, and that was fair enough—the last thing he wanted was involvement of an emotional kind with any woman—but that didn't mean they couldn't enjoy each other's company, did it?

Enjoy each other's company? The voice at the back of his head mocked him viciously. Why not be honest and admit what you mean? it challenged forcefully. You want her, you've lusted after her since the minute you set eyes on her, maybe just because she *is* so different from what you normally go for, with her fragile beauty and childish dusting of freckles.

Oh, to hell with it. He had never gone in for self-psychoanalysis and he didn't intend to start now, Jared thought irritably. There was nothing special about Henrietta Noake; she was just a woman like any other. He gave a mental nod of affirmation at the thought and cleared his mind with a ruthlessness Sandra Noake would have admired.

'Don't doubt it.' Jared stepped close to her now, and his voice was low and cool. 'The first thing you've got to get into your head in this dog-eat-dog world is that you're better than the rest. It's the only way to get to the top.'

'Perhaps I don't think it's that important to get to the top.' Henrietta was desperately aware of his great height and the overall *maleness* of him as she raised her chin, an uncomfortable tightness in her chest making it difficult to breathe.

'Then you won't,' he said flatly, one eyebrow raised derisively.

'Maybe not.' She suddenly felt in control for the first time that day and it was a good feeling. 'But wherever I am, I'll enjoy being there. Can you say that?' she asked perkily.

'Me?' She had hit a nerve and she knew it; it was visible in the tightening of that hard, sensual mouth and the way his eyes had narrowed into blue glass. 'We aren't discussing me.'

'Maybe we should.' She smiled serenely.

'Okay, over dinner, then,' he agreed without a moment's pause.

The sereneness vanished. 'I don't think so.' Henrietta made the mistake of glancing down, and her eyes became fixed on the open-necked blue shirt he was wearing, or, more precisely, the crisp black hair that was just visible in the V. He had been wearing a tie when he'd first come in—she was sure of it—but some time during the conversation with her mother the tie had vanished, and with it a certain element of refinement.

He would be an earthy lover. The thought came from nowhere along with a tingling hotness deep in the base of her stomach.

Uncivilised even, and certainly sensual. That one kiss all those weeks ago had told her he was a man who would take what he wanted, how he wanted and when he wanted from the partner of his choice. There would be no please and thank you, not with Jared Vincent. And yet she couldn't see him being rough. Erotic maybe, perhaps even lascivious, but his male authority would be tempered with sensitivity towards the woman he was bedding...

She emerged from the fascinating and dangerous area her thoughts had taken her into with a little shock of awareness at how much her mind had wandered, when Jared's voice, soft and silky, said, 'You can't stay in your ivory tower for ever, Henrietta. There's a big wide world out there, and sooner or later you will have to take the plunge again and start to live.'

'You're accusing me of not living because I won't come out to dinner with you?' she asked stiffly, still shaken by the sexual nature of her musings.

'Yes, I think I am.' He reached out a big hand and lifted her chin with one finger, looking deep into her eyes. 'What other reason is there?'

'Plenty, as it happens, and—'

'Here am I, alone in the big city on business and with nights to kill in the anonymity of a faceless hotel room, and you are denying me companionship,' he continued sadly, as though she hadn't spoken. 'Now, you're not an unkind or ungenerous person, I know that much about you, so it must be fear that's preventing you from accepting a perfectly straightforward invitation from a friend.'

'Fear?' Henrietta couldn't believe her ears. 'And since when have you been a friend?' she added ungraciously.

'Not a friend?' He quirked a wicked eyebrow. 'You see me as something other than a friend, Henrietta? What...exactly?'

'I don't see you as anything,' she retorted somewhat ridiculously, 'and I'm certainly not frightened of you.' A little dart of conscience pierced her and she shrugged it away as she continued, 'It's just that I'm staying with my brother and his family at the moment, and it would be rude to accept a dinner invitation when David is expecting me to go home with him. I don't see the children much as it is, and Murphy is waiting—'

She caught herself abruptly. What was she *doing*? She didn't have to explain anything to him, and he was making her babble like a lunatic. She had to calm down and take control again.

'Did I catch my name there?' She hadn't noticed David approaching, but as he joined them, slipping an arm round Henrietta's waist, she'd never been so glad to see her brother in all her life.

'I asked Henrietta out to dinner, but she explained your children would be disappointed if she accepted,' Jared said evenly, adding, 'Murphy too,' with a straight face as he glanced at Henrietta's pink cheeks.

'She's right.' Henrietta's love for her brother increased a hundredfold. 'But there's no reason why you can't join us if you don't mind a spot of bedlam,' David continued cheerfully.

Henrietta suddenly remembered all the times David had pulled her hair and teased her when she was little, and why she had hated him so passionately at fairly frequent intervals throughout their childhood.

'I couldn't impose on your wife like that.'

He was merely being polite, and when David said, 'Oh, Sarah's used to people popping in all the time; she'd love to see you, I promise, wouldn't she, Hen?' she knew protest was useless. 'Hen?' David nudged her with his elbow.

'Yes.' Henrietta forced a smile that was frayed round the edges. 'Sarah won't mind.'

'Then I'd love to come.' Jared smiled the smile Henrietta was learning he kept for special occasions, and this time there was a definite element of triumph in its toothpaste-commercial brightness.

'Here, I'll write down our address for you.' David was like a dog with two tails and Henrietta could almost see the pound signs in his eyes. 'It's the least we can do after you've been so generous this afternoon, and who would have thought Henrietta's landlord would be here today?' he said brightly.

Who indeed? Henrietta thought testily. Who indeed?

'I've thoroughly enjoyed it,' Jared murmured contentedly. 'I hadn't seen any of Henrietta's work before, but it's excellent; she has hidden depths. I'm looking forward to unearthing more in the future,' he added with an innocence that didn't fool Henrietta.

'Well, you're welcome to call in at the gallery or the shop any time,' David said earnestly. 'We always have some of Henrietta's pieces on show, and she is beginning to sell really well.'

'I'd certainly buy her any time,' Jared nodded seriously.

She'd had enough of this. Couldn't David *see* what he meant? Henrietta asked herself furiously. Or—and here Henrietta's assurance faltered and all the old doubts and insecurities from her time with Melvyn kicked in—was she putting two and two together and making ten?

And then she looked up into Jared's dancing eyes, and in spite of herself a glimmer of a smile touched her soft lips before she forced them into a severe line. He was dreadful, she thought firmly, and he didn't need any encouragement. Poor David—what would her brother say if he knew he had just been discussing Jared's hopes of seducing his baby sister?

'Come about eight?' Jared nodded in acknowledgement, and David's eyes glanced towards the door as he said, 'See you later, then; I've just got to catch Mrs deFischel before she goes. She owns a chain of shops in the West End...' And he dashed off to gush over a pink-haired, gaunt scarecrow of a woman who was dressed in Dior and diamonds with the obligatory white poodle under her arm.

'I don't know why she came.' Henrietta's gaze had followed David to the door, and now Jared turned to watch the little scenario being played out a few yards away. 'She's not into the sort of things I do; it's more sculptures and modern art with her. She adored Melvyn's work...' Her voice trailed away as she realised it was the first time she had voluntarily mentioned her husband's name since he had died. She waited for the rush of guilt and anguish that always accompanied the mildest thought of Melvyn, but it didn't come. Instead there was a deep, deep sadness.

'He was an artist?' Jared asked softly. His eyes had switched to her face but she wasn't aware of his glance as she watched David flatter the old woman.

'A sculptor. He was brilliant,' she said flatly. Brilliant and unbalanced. But then perhaps all geniuses were only a step away from madness? It was a thought she'd had more than once since his death.

'You can't live in the past, Henrietta.' Jared's voice brought her eyes to his. 'You're alive and he is dead,' he said with a baldness he hadn't intended. 'Sooner or later you have to pick yourself up and go forward.'

'I know that.' She resented him for the ease with which he said it. What did he know of the nightmare that had been her marriage? she asked herself silently. And she *was* forging her own destiny—this exhibition bore testimony to that.

'Do you? Do you really?' he asked urgently.

'Yes.' She lifted her chin in a gesture of dismissive defiance.

'Then why did you say you wanted to be left alone that night?' he asked huskily. He hadn't meant to say it; in fact he didn't know why he was saying it now. Since reaching adulthood, he had lived his life the way *he* wanted it, by his own moral code and his own principles, and they didn't include entanglements that had the slightest chance of getting messy.

'Because it was true—it *is* true.' The slip terrified her and now her voice was crisp. 'I know exactly what I want from life,' she said sharply.

Jared expelled a quiet breath, and then let his instinct take over as he took her by the arms, drawing her against him. 'I don't believe that,' he said softly, feeling her tremble as his body touched hers. 'You might think you do, but you're fooling yourself, Henrietta. You're warm and beautiful and *alive*, and there's more to life than your pots and painting and a Lady of the Lake existence.' He bent his head, allowing his lips to brush hers for a brief moment before he put her from him, walking straight to the door without glancing at her again.

She was shaking for some minutes after he had left, her lips still feeling the warmth of his and her senses caught up with the male life force that was so strong and intoxicatingly virile.

He was a charismatic man, she told herself tremblingly after she had escaped into the tiny cloakroom at the back of the gallery. That was all it was. He had a magnetism that was enhanced by his height and his overall maleness— some of the stars of the silver screen had the same indefinable something too which set them apart from the crowd. And it was attractive, she couldn't deny that, but it didn't *mean* anything, not really.

'Oh…' She leant against the clean, linen-papered wall as she groaned softly in her throat and shut her eyes tightly. She wished she had never gone to Herefordshire, she wished she had never set eyes on the mill, and most of all she wished Jared Vincent had never come into her life. And somehow, and she still wasn't quite sure how it had all come about, he was having dinner with her family tonight.

CHAPTER FIVE

'THAT was a wonderful meal, Sarah.' Jared leant back in his seat and smiled *that* smile at her sister-in-law as Henrietta looked on with something akin to disbelief. He had won them all over, she thought helplessly. He had set out to charm and ensnare from the moment he had arrived on the doorstep with arms full of wine and chocolates and flowers for the ladies.

And her sister-in-law—her shrewd, capable and very forthright sister-in-law—had been putty in his hands from the first few minutes. Even the children had taken to him big time before they had gone up to bed, the two older little girls acting the coquettes as they giggled and whispered behind their hands, and the younger two children, little Amy and Mark, clambering all over him and acting as though they'd known him all their lives.

Only Murphy wasn't having any of it. Henrietta glanced across to where the big dog was lying across the threshold of the room, his massive head between his huge front paws and his wise brown eyes fixed unblinkingly on Jared.

When the four adults had gone through to the dining room to eat—the children having been fed earlier and now in bed—Murphy had followed silently, flopping down in the doorway and refusing to move.

He was looking out for her, Henrietta thought with a burst of love for the faithful animal. He wasn't taken in by a charming manner and talk of friendship. Friendship! She almost snorted at the notion. A woman might be able to have a platonic friendship with a male colleague at work, or her grocer, or even an ex-boyfriend on occasion. But Jared Vincent? Never.

Henrietta was suddenly aware that Jared's gaze had switched to her, and she quickly schooled all trace of her thoughts from her face as she forced a bright smile and said, 'Sarah's a terrific cook. David is a very lucky man.'

'I know it.' David nodded contentedly as he patted his stomach, his self-satisfied expression wavering slightly when his wife flicked at him with her hand and demanded his presence in the kitchen without delay.

'I'll help you with the dishes, Sarah.' Henrietta was halfway to her feet before Sarah's protest stopped her.

'No way.' Everyone knew when Sarah meant what she said. 'You stay and talk to Jared for a while while we load the dishwasher and clean up a bit in there, and we'll bring coffee through shortly. Go and sit in the lounge; the French windows are still open into the garden and it's a lovely evening. I can't believe this warm spell is going to last much longer.'

It was hopeless. Everyone was in league against her. Henrietta slanted a glance at Jared's smug face and conceded defeat. But this was still tons better than an intimate dinner for two.

'How long have they been married?' Contrary to Henrietta's expectations Jared didn't press his advantage once they were in the other room, only raising his eyebrows fractionally as she made for a chair rather than the deep, plushly upholstered corner-style settee that stretched halfway round the room and was built to accommodate several people.

'Ten years. David married her when he was eighteen and Sarah was seventeen,' Henrietta answered carefully. She didn't want him to know too much about her family—she didn't want to form any links, however tenuous, with this man.

'That's very young.' He frowned slightly before clearing his expression almost immediately and saying, 'They must have been confident about how they felt to commit themselves like that?'

'Yes, I suppose so.' Henrietta's expressions revealed she didn't want to discuss this further, and her tone was dismissive when she said, 'It's worked out wonderfully anyway; they're as much in love now as when they first got married.'

'The exception that proves the rule,' Jared stated drily.

'That's a bit cynical,' Henrietta began, before she checked herself abruptly. Who was she to talk? she asked herself honestly. If Jared didn't believe in happy-ever-afters she was the last person in the world to argue with him.

'Possibly.' Jared nodded slowly, and then, as he glanced out into the shadowed garden which was nothing more than a square of lawn surrounded by trees and strategically placed bushes Sarah had chosen for their sweet scents, he said, 'Let's sit out there in the fresh air for a moment or two, unless you have any objection? I love this time of evening.'

There was a slight challenge in the words and Henrietta rose to it, her tone stiff as she said, 'Of course not, although they'll be coming through with the coffee soon.'

'At which point we can join them.' It was said in the soothing tones in which one would reassure a child, and made Henrietta hopping mad. He thought she was nervous about being alone with him out there? Think on, Jared Vincent, she told him silently as she followed him out into the dusky darkness which was as warm and fragrant as any summer's evening.

There was only one small wooden bench in a far corner of the lawn, and when Henrietta sat at Jared's prompting and he joined her a moment later she felt her heart jump into her throat as his thigh wedged against hers. He was wearing that same aftershave she had liked before, its sharp, slightly lemony overtones producing a sensual scent when mixed with the chemicals in his cool tanned skin, and she felt her stomach muscles contract as he turned towards her, sliding one arm along the back of the bench as he shifted on the small seat. Henrietta suddenly found she couldn't breathe.

'This is nice,' he murmured easily. 'The house was a little stuffy, don't you think?'

What she was thinking didn't bear scrutiny.

'You were right in there when you called me cynical,' Jared said after a long electric moment when Henrietta felt her nerve-endings twang and scream. 'But I don't think that's necessarily a bad thing, do you?' he asked softly.

'Me? I...I don't know.' She didn't know anything with the feel of his body all around her, and concentrated very hard on staring at the small birdbath some feet away. She had changed out of her suit and high-heeled shoes once she had got home, and was now clad in a plain blue, knitted wool dress, her hair loose about her shoulders. She had purposely not dressed up, neither had she renewed her make-up. She would *not* titivate for Jared Vincent.

'I think cynicism is just another word for awareness,' he continued evenly, 'and that can begin at any age, depending on circumstances.'

'And with you it was early.' It was more of a statement than a question, but he nodded anyway.

'My mother died when I was born,' he said unemotionally, 'and as I was an only child that meant a pretty isolated childhood. My father never married again, although he had a succession of...relationships, most of them not lasting more than a few months. He wasn't good at communicating—in fact he was lousy at it—but we got on all right most of the time at a surface level, mainly because he was never around, I guess. And then I hit eighteen.'

Henrietta was aware she was hearing bare facts that covered up a great deal and also that he had probably never talked about this before, and her voice was quiet when she said, 'What happened when you were eighteen?'

'I met a girl.' He smiled mirthlessly. 'The love of my life—you know how it is when you are eighteen. I met her on my first day at university and she came home with me for the Christmas holidays after I'd told my father how madly in love we were.'

'And your father didn't approve of her?' Henrietta asked carefully. She could imagine Jared's father would have been very wary regarding any liaison his son had, knowing that there were women who would be attracted as much by the Vincent name, and the power and wealth it embodied, as by his son.

'Oh, he approved of her.' There was a note in his voice that caused her gaze to swing to his face, but he was staring out over the sleeping garden now, and the hard, dim profile was shadowed and told her nothing. 'He very much approved of her.'

'You mean…?' She didn't know quite how to go on.

'And *she* liked what he could buy for her,' Jared continued harshly. 'I think my father used her as an object lesson to teach me that everyone has their price. I learnt the lesson well.'

'I don't believe that…that everyone can be bought,' Henrietta objected quickly, more horrified than she dared express at what he had confided. How could a father—*a father*—do something like that? It was one thing to be emotionally cold to your son, as Jared's father obviously had been all through Jared's childhood, but to sleep with your son's first real love? To steal her away and flaunt her? That was sick, disgusting. What must it have done to the young Jared, already starved of love and affection for all his life? she asked herself silently.

Jared shrugged, his voice steady and revealing nothing of what he was feeling as he said, 'Like I said, there is always the exception that proves the rule.'

'How long did…did it go on?' Henrietta asked tentatively.

'Some months; my father's lovers never lasted longer than that. He bought her off with a sports car and one or two other tasty trinkets, and they parted fairly amicably, so I understand. She lived at Fotheringham while the affair was at its height and then disappeared. I heard from a mutual friend that she got a place at another university the following year. She was a survivor,' he finished with the first trace of bitterness.

So, that was the reason for his long absences from Fotheringham. The place must reek of memories he'd rather forget. For the first time since Melvyn's death Henrietta took a mental step backwards and realised her thirteen months of misery, bad though they had been, had been mercifully short in the overall span of her life.

She wanted to cry for the lonely, lost little boy growing up in the great mausoleum of a house that was Fotheringham, brushed aside—if not ignored—by the person who should have been closest to him. What havoc had been wrought on a young, fertile mind by the severity of the betrayal? she asked herself silently. It was bad enough that his girlfriend had been lured away, but that it was his own father who had done the tempting—it didn't bear thinking about.

'Did you discuss her with your father, after she had gone?'

'No.' Jared looked at her now, and the blue eyes were uncompromisingly cold. 'We communicated only by telephone from that initial Christmas at Fotheringham until the day he died. He never asked to see me to explain anything, and I never suggested it.'

Why, *why* had he told her all this? It had destroyed all the preconceived ideas she had had of him—*needed* to have. She didn't want to see him as a vulnerable, flesh-and-blood human being who was capable of feeling hurt and pain and loss. It was dangerous, it was just too dangerous, and she didn't *want* to analyse why.

'I'm so sorry, Jared.' And she was, heart-sorry.

'I don't know why I told you all this.' There was a faint note of bewilderment in his grim voice that made Henrietta feel he was telling the truth, and that added to her turmoil.

'Perhaps...perhaps it was just time to tell somebody?' she suggested faintly, and then, as her eyes caught and held his, she murmured, 'Jared, no...'

The kiss wasn't at all like the one so many weeks before. As he crushed her into him there was an urgency, a savagery about his embrace that sent a flood of heady sensation spiralling through her even as she fought against its potent power.

His body was hard against hers, and the shadowed garden—with its scents and cosmopolitan echoes from the world outside its walls—simply melted away.

His mouth was deep and consuming, its erotic assault fiery, and as he pressed her into the hard wood she didn't even feel the bench beneath her softness. He was trembling, she could feel it, and somehow that released an exultant primitive response that was like a drug as she realised the cool control had all but vanished.

And then, as suddenly as he had taken hold of her, she was free. He was breathing harshly as he got to his feet, and his voice was ragged as he said, 'We'd better go in, Henrietta.'

'Yes…' She couldn't move. She wanted to, she really wanted to, if only to show him she could call on the sort of discipline he was displaying, but her legs felt like jelly and her head was literally spinning. It was humiliating and embarrassing and a hundred other things besides, but there it was.

'I somehow suspect your brother and his wife would object to finding us *in flagrante delicto* under the apple blossom?' Jared continued softly as he turned to face her, his blue eyes gleaming like a great cat's in the dim light.

'I hardly think that was a possibility,' she managed shakily.

'No?' His gaze caught and pinned her down. 'I don't know whether to be pleased or insulted at your faith in my ability to stop,' he said silkily, one eyebrow quirking.

She stared at him without moving or speaking. There had been a mocking element to his last words she didn't like, but it cut through the residue of weakness and swept it away like magic. 'It wasn't *your* ability to stop I was referring to,' Henrietta said stonily, the heat draining from her face and leaving it chalk-white.

Why was he behaving like this? As though he had to belittle the overwhelming, phenomenal *event* of that kiss? She had never, in all her wildest imaginings, dreamed up a kiss with the mind-blowing power of that one they had just shared. Did he kiss all his women like that? The thought hurt more than she would have thought possible, and doused the last remnant of tenderness his revelation about his father had produced.

'And you're wrong,' she heard herself saying in the next instant before she could take hold of her tongue and quell the hurt and humiliation. 'There is a huge difference between cynicism and awareness. The former is a result of a human being becoming stunted and distorted emotionally, while the latter is simply another word for wisdom. They are quite, quite different.'

'You think so,' he said grimly, his voice very controlled, but Henrietta knew she had made him angry and she didn't care one jot. If nothing else she was going to be honest, she thought determinedly. She hadn't asked him to share his past with her—he had volunteered it—and if he wanted someone to tickle his ears and tell him only what he wanted to hear he'd better call on one of his girlfriends.

'Hen? Are you out there?'

As Sarah's voice called out into the night the rattle of coffee cups followed, and then her sister-in-law appeared in the lighted doorway of the French windows with David just behind her. It was a picture of togetherness and made everything worse.

'Just coming.' Jared recovered more quickly than Henrietta, his voice perfectly normal as he called back. 'Henrietta and I were just taking a breath of fresh air; it's lovely out here and some of these scents are wonderful. Is that a little herb garden to one side of the windows?'

They had been walking back towards the house as Jared spoke and now, as Sarah began to tell him about the herbs which were her pride and joy, Henrietta found herself watching them. A few moments ago his heart had been pounding like a sledge-hammer, and she had been held so close to that hard male frame she had felt every inch of his body as he had moulded her into him. He had been aroused—hugely—and he had wanted her. And before that, when he had told her about his childhood and his university girlfriend, he had been yet another Jared Vincent, and had called forth a different set of emotions in her, different but still dangerous.

And now? Now it was the man the rest of the world saw—the cool, charming, wealthy businessman and country squire in perfect control of his life and his future.

And what did people see when they looked at her? she asked herself in the next instant, her gaze on Sarah's animated face but her mind a million miles away. A capable young widow, probably, someone who had coped well with the tragedy that had befallen her and was making a success of her career in spite of everything that had happened. They had no idea, either, about her or Jared's shocking history. How many other people were covering up heartache and damage with a bright face and a determined smile? Thousands—millions—but that didn't help her right now.

But one thing was for sure. Her eyes narrowed, the pupils dilating and making her velvet brown gaze even darker. She and Jared couldn't

be worse for each other. If he was ever to put
the past behind him, and perhaps that was impossible, he would need someone like Sarah—
uncomplicated, bouncy, easygoing, with no
traumatic background of her own—to give him
faith in love and life again. And she? She didn't
know what she needed, but it certainly wasn't
Jared Vincent.

Oh, what was she going on like this for anyway? she chided herself irritably. There wasn't
the faintest possibility she and Jared would ever
have even the most fleeting relationship; they
both knew that at heart. He was—what? Thirty-
six or thirty-seven, Mrs Baker had thought—and
used to a lifestyle that would make it difficult
to accommodate any woman on a permanent ba-
sis, and that was the way he liked it. His sort of
woman was the Anastasia type—cool, beautiful
women who knew the score and how to play the
game.

So why had he got under her skin so strongly?
She frowned in frustration. She didn't know, but
she wished she could do what that old song had
suggested and wash him out of her hair. He
made everything so…complicated.

Jared stayed for another hour—an hour that
the other three seemed to find most enjoyable
and Henrietta endured with gritted teeth as she

smiled and chatted as though she hadn't a care in the world.

When at last he rose to leave, Henrietta sprang up with an alacrity that, too late, she realised David and Sarah had misunderstood as her sister-in-law said, with a little conspiratorial smile and nod, 'You can see Jared to the door, can't you, Hen, while David and I take these things through to the kitchen?'

Oh, they thought she wanted to be alone with him for a few minutes, Henrietta thought helplessly as her cheeks glowed scarlet. It didn't help that Jared's wicked blue eyes were expressing amusement at her discomfiture, either, and she almost hustled him out of the room, praying he would make a quick exit and she could return immediately to her brother and his wife to kill any notions of a lingering farewell.

'Calm down.' The cool amusement did *nothing* to calm her.

'What?' Her voice was too sharp and she tried to moderate it a tone or two as she said, 'I don't understand what you mean.'

'You're like a cat on a hot tin roof, woman.' He leant back against the wall at the side of the door as though he had all the time in the world, and Henrietta's frustration grew.

'I am not.' She glared at him. 'It's just that…'

'Yes?' He crossed his arms leisurely. 'What is it exactly?'

'They think…'

'Spit it out, Henrietta. What do they think?' he asked mildly.

He was enjoying this, she thought feverishly. She could see it in his face. He knew *exactly* how she felt. 'They think that we're…interested in each other,' she managed at last, her face threatening to explode in flames, 'and I don't like it that they've got the wrong idea.'

'They haven't as far as I'm concerned,' he said calmly, 'but then we've already established that. I *am* interested in you, Henrietta—I'm very interested,' he said pleasantly.

'You're talking about sex.' And then she stared at him, horrified, as she heard the echo of what she had said. But he'd provoked her into that, she told herself furiously. He was the most *irritating* man she had ever met in all her life.

'Henrietta, I'm surprised at you.' The blue eyes danced as he shook his head gravely. 'How very carnal. I had no idea your mind ran along such lines.'

'Look, Jared—' She stopped abruptly, taking a deep breath and willing herself to calm down. She had to spell it out—say it as it was. It was the only way with a man like him. 'I…I need to make something very clear,' she said hollowly, hoping she could put this in the right way. She didn't want to hurt him, she realised suddenly. 'I don't want to get involved with a man at the moment, be it friendship or anything else.' She gulped deep in her throat as his thoughtful expression didn't change. 'It's not you, not really, it's just that I'm happy as I am,' she continued bravely, 'although of course our lifestyles are worlds apart.'

'No, they're not.' He didn't move a muscle, his eyes intent on her troubled face. 'You've got a career you enjoy and you're good at; so have I. You put all the hours under the sun into your work; so do I. You don't want anything heavy emotionally, and I've never been any good at commitment and roses-round-the-door-type relationships. I'd say we were perfectly suited.'

'No, we're not.' She stared at him in frustration. '*I* wouldn't be any good at an affair; I know I wouldn't. I'm not built that way. Mel…Melvyn was the first man I'd slept with, and—' she hesitated, and then decided she might as well say it all '—and I didn't even particularly like that side of marriage.'

'Then he wasn't doing it right,' Jared said imperturbably, his voice as matter-of-fact as if they were discussing the weather or the cricket score.

'You're not frigid, Henrietta, if that's what you're suggesting. In fact I'd say you are one passionate lady under that prim, touch-me-not exterior.'

'*Jared.*' She glanced nervously back along the hall. They were in her brother's house for goodness' sake; he shouldn't be saying things like this to her. Didn't he care that David and Sarah might hear? she asked herself feverishly.

Apparently not. 'You want me, Henrietta, and we both know it. And I want you. It's really very simple and straightforward,' Jared said softly. 'You're free and so am I, and neither of us is inexperienced. So what's stopping us enjoying each other?'

Everything. Absolutely everything. 'Please go, Jared.' She wanted to cry, and set her face all the more because of it, her eyes veiled. She could hear Murphy whining and scratching behind the closed dining room door, and now she added, 'I've got to see to Murphy; I'm sorry—'

'And it's not just sex.' As she made to turn his voice brought her back to face him again. 'I like your company, Henrietta, and I enjoy being with you. We strike sparks off each other, don't we? Our time together wouldn't be boring,' he murmured wryly.

She had prayed for boring when she was with Melvyn. Prayed for it, longed for it, *craved* it amidst the violent, tumultuous storm her life had become. Boring she could live with; it was the other side of the coin that still filled her with terror in the middle of the night when she awoke from a nightmare and believed—just for a moment—that she was still married.

'Goodbye, Jared.' She looked him straight in the face now and there was something in her eyes that caused him to lever himself off the wall, his gaze narrowing.

'Is that your final word?' he asked quietly, already knowing the answer.

She nodded, not trusting herself to speak.

'I don't like it,' he said softly, with the glimmer of a smile, 'but then you didn't expect me to, did you?'

'Jared—'

'It's too harsh, too unkind a word,' he continued slowly as he reached out and took her into his arms, kissing her with an intensity and a sweetness that caused the tears to scald her closed eyelids. His fingers tangled in the silky curls of her hair as his hands pulled her closer, and it wasn't until he felt her lips quiver and open beneath his, allowing him access into the sweet secret places, that he let her go.

'Much too unkind.' He kissed the tip of her nose as she opened her eyes in surprise and then he was gone, the door closing quietly behind him as she continued to stand without speaking, her thought processes numbed and her resolve shattered.

And then she leapt towards the door, calling to him as she stepped hastily outside, 'I mean it, Jared.' Her voice was breathless as she watched him turn to face her, his face shadowed. 'I don't want to give you the wrong impression and I haven't changed my mind.'

'I know,' he affirmed slowly.

'And I shan't in the future,' she said more strongly.

'Maybe.' The deep male voice was cool and unconcerned. 'But for now it's late and you've had an exhausting day. Go to bed, Henrietta.'

She watched him walk away without saying anything further but as she turned to re-enter the house Henrietta felt more troubled than she had felt since the terrible aftermath of Melvyn's death.

CHAPTER SIX

HENRIETTA awoke early the next day in David and Sarah's little boxroom, golden stripes of sunshine from the half-open blinds at the window falling on her face and Murphy's snores—from his position at the side of the bed where he had slept quite contentedly on his blankets—loud in the quietness of the spring morning.

She hadn't slept well; it had been gone three before she had drifted into a troubled, restless sleep and even then she had dozed most of the time, tossing and turning as Murphy's snores had reverberated in her ears.

Had she done the right thing? It was something she had asked herself a hundred times since Jared had left the night before, but each time she had arrived at the same conclusion—she had done the only thing possible for her self-preservation. She had had no choice, not really. And she was tired—bone-tired—of self-analysis.

She climbed out of bed, stepping over Murphy who opened one eye and then snuggled down into his blankets again at her, 'Stay, boy,' and padded into the bathroom at the end of the landing. Her pink-rimmed eyes bore evidence to the bout of crying the night before, and her hair hung limp and lank about her pale face.

Right. She took stock and raised her chin determinedly. A warm shower with that expensive shower gel her mother had bought her for Christmas, and she'd condition her hair too. And then plenty of body lotion and even a manicure? She glanced down at her nails, which always suffered as a result of her craft, and nodded to herself. Yes, definitely a manicure. She was going to look good today if it killed her. She had three more days in London before she was due to go back to Herefordshire, and she wasn't going to spend them moping, however she felt deep inside.

Yesterday had been her 'official' on-duty stint at the exhibition and she intended to pop into the gallery a few more times over the next three days, but this morning she had promised Murphy a long walk in Hyde Park, and that was exactly what he was going to get. The weather forecasts had predicted the current warm spell was due to end tomorrow, heralding storms and a rainy spell, so today she and Murphy would make hay while the sun shone.

She was a long time in the bathroom but when she emerged, creamed and conditioned and perfumed, she felt a bit better, at least physically.

She dressed casually in grey leggings and boots teamed with a long cream jumper, looping her hair high on her head in a silky ponytail and only bothering with the merest touch of make-up in the form of mascara. Tiny gold studs in her ears and a dab of perfume at her wrists and she was ready for breakfast.

So was Murphy. There had been bacon cooking downstairs for the last ten minutes if he wasn't much mistaken, and his mouth was watering.

Murphy had a good breakfast—most of it secreted to him under the table by Henrietta, who found she couldn't eat a thing. But she was fine—*fine*, she told herself firmly. Totally, one-hundred-per-cent fine. Everything was just great.

The telephone rang at half past eight just as David had flown out of the door and Sarah had gone to chivvy up her little chicks, who were due at school and nursery, so Henrietta picked it up, stating the number quietly.

'Henrietta?'

The deep, husky voice brought her hand fluttering to her throat in shock and caused her heart to gallop, and she found she couldn't say a word.

'Hello? Henrietta, is that you?' Jared's voice was slightly impatient now, and she forced herself to answer after another long moment of silence.

'Yes, this is me,' she mumbled ungrammatically, before taking a hold on herself and saying more firmly as she lied through her teeth, 'I'm sorry, I had a mouthful of bacon.'

'Right.' Jared's voice was brisk. 'Look, my meeting has been cancelled this morning so I've got some extra time to kill. What are your plans today?'

Her plans today? Henrietta moved the phone from her ear and stared at it in sheer disbelief. *Her plans?* Was he stupid or what? She had spent a terrible night doing endless postmortems and here he was, bright-eyed and bushy-tailed, asking her what her plans were? She didn't believe him; she really didn't.

'I'm busy,' she stated flatly.

'Doing what?'

'Things…'

'Could you be more specific?' he asked reasonably.

Henrietta tried a different approach. 'Jared, I thought we got all this straightened out last night,' she said firmly, and then, as Sarah popped her head round the kitchen door and called, 'Anyone for me, Hen?' called back, 'No, it's no one, Sarah.'

'Charming.' The male voice was very dry.

'Sarah wondered if it was someone for her,' Henrietta explained hastily, and then wondered why she was bothering to soothe his ruffled feathers. She didn't want to appease him for goodness' sake. He had to get the message, didn't he?

'Come out to lunch with me.' There was a note of stubbornness that made Henrietta wrinkle her brow in frustration. And then, before she could answer, he said, 'I promise I won't mention the S word, how about that? This will just be two friends from the same place meeting in a foreign land and keeping each other company. No strings, I promise.'

'Jared, I'm a Londoner for goodness' sake.'

'Ah, but you're living in Herefordshire now so it doesn't count,' he said triumphantly.

'No.' She gripped the phone more firmly. 'I meant what I said last night. There's just no point, don't you see?'

'No, I don't,' he answered smartly, 'so convince me. Meet me for lunch and convince me.'

Oh, this was ridiculous! If she were on her own she'd put the phone down, but knowing Jared he would ring straight back if she did that, and Henrietta didn't want David and Sarah knowing about her decision not to see him again. They had been positively babbling with enthusiasm about him last night, and she just couldn't take the sort of questions her brother would throw at her if she told him she had committed the unforgivable sin of slighting a potentially very juicy source of revenue for the business.

Jared had already promised David he would mention the gallery and the shop to some of his friends and business colleagues, and David had been beside himself with delight. As Jared had known he would be, of course—he was nothing if not a brilliant strategist, Henrietta thought nastily. No doubt he had summed David up within the first sixty seconds of meeting him.

'I'm not going to the gallery this morning actually,' Henrietta said coolly after a long moment of silence, 'and I shan't be suitably dressed to meet you anywhere for lunch. I've promised Murphy a long walk and I don't plan to get back till this afternoon.'

'No problem.' She'd won? 'I could do with blowing the cobwebs away; I'll come with you.' No, she hadn't.

Henrietta knew when she was beaten, but she still said, 'It might be a bit tiring for your leg; I plan to walk a long way. He was cooped up all yesterday and he needs a good run.'

'I think I can just about manage to keep up with you,' Jared said drily, 'in spite of my infirmity. I'll be round in about half an hour; is that all right?'

No, it was not all right and he damn well knew it. 'Fine.' It was a soft snarl and she thought she heard him chuckle before the phone went dead.

'Who was that?' From the way Sarah sprang out of the kitchen the moment the phone went down Henrietta had the feeling her sister-in-law knew exactly who she had been speaking to.

'Jared.' Prevarication was useless. 'He's coming with me to take Murphy for a walk,' Henrietta said flatly.

'You don't sound too thrilled about it,' Sarah stated questioningly. 'Is anything wrong?'

Henrietta shrugged, and then, as her sister-in-law touched her arm, her eyes soft with enquiry, said, 'Between ourselves, Sarah? Just you and me?'

'My lips will be sealed,' Sarah agreed seriously. 'Even if David applies the old water torture treatment I won't give in.'

Henrietta poked her in the ribs as she smiled, but then her face straightened. 'I don't want to get involved in a relationship, Sarah. Not with Jared Vincent, not with any man, but he just won't accept that I mean what I say.'

'That's because he isn't just "any man".' Sarah looked at Henrietta soberly. 'You'd go a long, long way before you found another like him.'

'I don't want another like him—I don't even want *him*.' Henrietta wasn't at all sure that was true, and it made her voice all the more vehement as she added, 'I'm not ready for a relationship, Sarah. I don't know if I will ever be ready.'

'Hen…' Sarah paused. She wasn't the type of person to barge in where angels feared to tread, but she loved her sister-in-law and had been grieved both by the fact that her marriage clearly hadn't been a bed of roses, and that the circumstances of Melvyn's death had made it all the more difficult for Henrietta in the caustic aftermath of the funeral. 'I know things weren't good between you and Melvyn before he died from the little you told us after he suggested that awful operation, and I know David feels guilty that he didn't take more notice at the time. But all men aren't like Melvyn.'

'I know that, in here.' Henrietta touched her forehead with a weary hand. 'But in my heart I'm too scared to take the risk. And if I decide to date again it wouldn't be with a man like Jared. He's too strong, too charismatic, too…'

'Much like Melvyn?' Sarah finished for her. 'Hen, listen to me. He is *nothing* like Melvyn,' she said urgently.

'Anyway, he's only in the market for casual affairs,' Henrietta said quietly. 'He's already told me that, laid his rules out in the open as it were.'

'He has?' Sarah looked shocked.

'Uh-huh. Added to which he's got a pretty rough history himself to come to terms with; it would be like the blind leading the blind, Sarah. Whatever way you look at it it's no go.'

'Well, you know best.' Sarah stared at her, her pretty face regretful. 'But I would love to see you meet someone who really knows how to make you happy, Hen. Look, I've got to start the rat-run and get these kids to school and nursery. We're eating dinner at seven tonight, okay?'

'Okay.'

The two women hugged and then, after the whirlwind of the children and Sarah leaving, Henrietta was alone. She loaded the dishwasher, cleaned up the kitchen table where the children had breakfasted and wiped over the floor where Amy had spilt her milk, and then glanced down at Murphy who was sitting hopefully by the back door, reminding her quite pointedly of her promise.

'We're going, we're going.' She smiled at the big dog who looked like a wolf and was as gentle as a lamb. 'But we're not going to be alone on our walk.'

Murphy gave a woof of anticipation—his mistress had mentioned that magic word—but the intelligent brown eyes were enquiring as his massive head tilted to one side. There was something in her voice that worried him.

'Come on, let's give you a brush and then we'll put your collar on. How about that?' Henrietta said softly. 'And I want you to stick close today, okay? You're my official guardian angel.'

There was another deep woof before huge paws placed themselves on her shoulders and a long pink tongue licked her face, causing Henrietta to squeal and laugh as she pushed the dog down. How she would have got through the last year without him she didn't know; he was thirty-five kilograms of pure tonic as far as she was concerned.

However, she wasn't smiling some ten minutes later when she answered the door to Jared's authoritative knock.

'Good morning.' He looked wonderful, and Henrietta found her voice was slightly squeaky as she returned the greeting. He was dressed casually in black jeans and a charcoal denim shirt that was open at the neck. The sleeves were rolled up to just below his elbows and his forearms were muscled and hairy, emphasising the overall dark quality of his maleness. Normally he was intimidating enough; today he was positively threatening, and Henrietta needed the few seconds fussing with Murphy's lead to recover her shaky equilibrium.

She had purposely been ready for his knock and she didn't ask him in. A walk with Murphy and other people around was one thing—there was safety in numbers—but she didn't want to be alone with him, and as they turned to walk down the path leading out of David's nine feet or so of front garden Jared said, 'We'll go in my car, yes?' as he glanced at her little Mini parked in the street.

It made sense—once Murphy had scrambled into the back of the Mini it always seemed as if the car was overfull anyway as his head peered between the two front seats—but Henrietta would have preferred the initiative to remain with her. However, she forced a quick smile as she answered, 'Fine, thank you.'

It wasn't the Range Rover or the Ferrari that awaited them as they crossed the road to where Jared had parked, but a white BMW with pale blue upholstery that didn't look at all dog-proof.

'Are you sure you want Murphy in there?' Henrietta asked doubtfully as Jared opened the door. 'He might look all right now but he's still moulting like mad, and knowing Murphy he'll be muddy when we come back. I really don't think—'

'You worry too much.' The vivid blue eyes smiled at her. 'I've a load of blankets in the boot we can use if we need to, and I like dogs, Henrietta. They like me too—' he glanced at Murphy who was standing like a sentinel by Henrietta's side and the German shepherd stared back at him unblinkingly '—usually.'

'Well, if you're sure.' Be it on his own head. 'I'm sure.'

'Do you know how to get to Hyde Park?' Henrietta asked helpfully once they were on the move.

'Yes, but I think we can do a little better than Hyde Park, don't you?' Jared said imperturbably. 'A dog like Murphy needs open fields and real smells to wallow in. I know a couple of good walks on the outskirts from my university days, one of which has the added advantage of a good pub at the end of it. Leave it to me.'

She didn't like this. She didn't like it at all. 'Murphy would be quite happy in Hyde Park; there's really no need to go further afield,' Henrietta said warily.

He brushed aside the feeble protest. 'You said yourself the weather is going to break. At least give the poor animal a fair crack of the whip today,' he said reproachfully, as though she were the worst pet owner in the world.

Henrietta turned and looked at the poor animal who stared back at her, tongue lolling. You just make sure you stick to me like glue today, she told him silently, or else I'll have your guts for garters. This was all she needed, a quiet, romantic walk in rolling countryside with not another soul in sight.

As it happened, once they had reached their destination after a half-hour drive, parked the car in a secluded leafy lane and climbed a stile into green fields, Henrietta found she was thoroughly enjoying the day. Jared was showing yet another side to his—she was now realising— complicated personality, that of genial, witty and very amusing companion, his conversation easy and non-threatening, and his attitude that of a friend, nothing more. She didn't trust the metamorphosis, not for a second, but she was more than happy to go along with it in the circumstances.

The morning was a beautiful one, the cloudless blue sky and gentle warm breeze making each step a pleasure, and Murphy was having the time of his life, chasing first one delicious smell and then another as they tramped the signed footpaths through deserted countryside, where only the mooing of cows and bleating of sheep disturbed the tranquillity.

They reached the little thatched pub just after midday, and Henrietta was enchanted with the olde-worlde interior of low wooden beams and gleaming brasses that greeted them. When Murphy was established—with the landlord's permission—under their table, they sipped at foaming, ice-cold draught ale while they waited for their lunch of home-made steak and kidney pie to be served, the sharp, smooth taste of the ale just right after the long hot walk.

'Enjoying it?'

Jared smiled at her from his viewpoint across the table, his big body perfectly relaxed as he leant back in his seat and his heavily lashed eyes piercingly blue as they crinkled at the corners.

'Very much.' Too much. 'Did you come here often when you were a student?' she asked carefully, aware that in the last few seconds something had shifted and the atmosphere was tightening. Perhaps it was something to do with the way he was looking at her, or maybe it was just that this cosy table for two, ensconced in a secluded corner, was a mite too intimate.

Whatever, she was suddenly uncomfortably aware of his unique brand of flagrant masculinity in a way she hadn't been on the relaxed walk here—the scent from his warm male skin, the blackness of his hair, the way his jeans pulled across hard-muscled thighs causing trouble with her breathing.

'Quite often.' He folded his arms over his chest, settling into his seat as he surveyed her with narrowed eyes. 'After the business with Candy—' so that had been her name—Candy, Henrietta thought musingly '—a group of friends rallied round. I think they thought I

needed distracting, and certainly after some of
the nights at university, which could get pretty
wild, a walk in the country did us all some
good.'

'Male and female friends?' It wasn't tactful
but she couldn't help asking and he could be
pretty inquisitive on occasion too.

'Uh-huh.' He eyed her expressionlessly.

'And the females joined in the distracting, I
suppose?' she asked lightly. 'I noticed there
were quite a few nice, secluded corn fields on
the way here.' Keep it casual, Hen, keep it casual.

'Did you, now?' He raked back a lock of hair
as he smiled lazily. 'Well, there were a few moments of ''distracting'' if I remember rightly,'
he agreed easily. 'Hot summer days, a bunch of
kids let loose for the first time in their lives with
no parental rules and regulations—you know
how it is.'

She didn't actually. Hers had been a particularly sheltered upbringing, and she had attended
college whilst still living at home with her
mother. David had married by then, and
Henrietta hadn't felt able to leave her mother all
alone so soon after the death of her husband.
She had never regretted the sacrifice, but she
had often wondered if she would have been

quite so blind to Melvyn's true nature if she had had the experience of spreading her wings before she met him.

'And you?' He leant forward suddenly, his eyes glittering. 'You said Melvyn was the fist guy you'd slept with, but you must have had boyfriends before him? Had fun?'

'Yes, I had a few boyfriends,' she said quietly. Fairly platonic relationships that hadn't touched either her heart or her senses, and which she had finished as soon as her beau had begun to get remotely serious. In fact by the time Melvyn had come along she had begun to wonder if there was something wrong with her. Several of her girlfriends had fallen in and out of love as regularly as clockwork, and she knew they'd considered it strange that she hadn't slept with any of her boyfriends.

But she had never felt that certain *something* which she was sure you were supposed to feel before you committed your heart and your body to someone. That something that David and Sarah had, and that her parents—unlike as they had been—had felt. And so she had waited, and Melvyn had exploded into her life with all the excitement and passion she could ever have hoped for…

'But you knew they weren't the right ones?' Jared persisted softly. 'Your other boyfriends?'

'I suppose so.' She nodded slowly, her eyes shadowed and remote. She had waited for the real thing, for love, and look where that had got her, she thought bitterly, before that other self—the self that had become more and more strong over the last year—said to her, You were right to wait. Okay, it didn't work out, it went horribly wrong, but you were still right to wait. *The breakdown of her marriage, and Melvyn's death, hadn't been her fault.*

She stared at Jared as the conviction reverberated in her head, filling her mind. A part of her—a large part—had never really fully accepted her role as innocent victim. It had been like a get-out clause in a dodgy court case, and her misplaced guilt and agony of mind had fed the notion. But she *had* been innocent. She had done everything she could—and then some more—to save her marriage. *It hadn't been her fault.*

'Henrietta?' Jared reached out and touched her arm, her white face and dazed expression concerning him. 'What is it?'

'Nothing.' She ignored the pounding of her heart and the faint, dizzy feeling the overwhelming relief had brought, and repeated, 'Nothing. I'm...I'm just ready for my lunch.'

The meal, when it came, was absolutely delicious and Henrietta ate every scrap, although she couldn't manage the sticky dessert that Jared consumed with relish.

'The food's just as good as I remember.' He had just finished the most enormous helping of treacle pudding and custard, and Henrietta found herself smiling at the overt satisfaction in his voice. 'We used to fill up here for the week— the meals at the student union were foul.'

'Jared...' Henrietta hesitated. She shouldn't be asking this because she really didn't know how to cope with the answer if it was in the negative. 'Did you really have your meeting cancelled today?' she said quietly.

'The meeting was cancelled, yes.' And then, as she nodded trustingly at his reply, he found himself admitting, 'I'm the chairman and managing director of the firm; I cancelled it.'

Henrietta stiffened, and now his voice was both soothing and reproachful as he said, 'You really left me with very little alternative, you know that, don't you? All that fierce aggression and distrust last night—what was a mere man to do? I like you, Henrietta—' Henrietta's stomach clenched against the soft, husky tones

'—and I wanted to spend some time with you. That's all.'

'It was dishonest.' She didn't trust the open, innocent expression on his face any more than she trusted him.

'No, not really. The meeting *was* cancelled.' He smiled disarmingly. 'You just didn't ask the right questions, that's all. I wouldn't have lied to you.'

'Huh.' She frowned at him, not at all mollified.

'And what would your answer have been if I had asked you to dinner tonight?'

'You know what it would have been,' she answered hotly.

'Exactly.' He shook his head complacently. 'I rest my case.'

'Jared, I don't like to be manipulated,' she said stonily. Melvyn had been a master of that particular exercise.

'Is that what I was doing?' He seemed genuinely surprised.

'Of course it was.' She found herself glaring at him, her colour high. 'And don't come the innocent with me either. You knew *exactly* what you were doing.'

'I don't suppose it would do me any good to plead extenuating circumstances?' he asked meekly.

'You suppose right.' She was trying, she was *really* trying to remain angry, but Jared Vincent in humble mode was hard to resist. And he *had* admitted to deceiving her when he needn't have done. 'Being economical with the truth is just as bad as an out-and-out lie, you know,' she said severely, her freckles glowing indignantly.

'I stand corrected,' he murmured softly. 'You see before you a penitent man.'

'A penitent man? Yes, right.' Her tone was sceptical, her mouth turned down at the corners with disapproval, and suddenly he laughed out loud, the sound almost rusty as though he didn't do it too often. Henrietta liked the sound.

'Henrietta Noake, you really are the most fascinating woman,' he murmured as she stared at him in surprise, 'but this honesty of yours takes a little getting used to. Do you always say exactly what you mean? Don't you ever flirt a little, tease, lead a man on?' he asked softly.

'Of course not.' She sounded quite horrified, and again the rasping chuckle sounded before he said, his tone mild but shaking with laugher, 'Of course not. A virtuous woman—well, well. Perhaps I should snatch you up and put you in a glass tower where the world can come and view such a phenomenon.'

'This is a very silly conversation,' Henrietta said haughtily, her face scarlet.

'You're quite right.' But refreshing, very refreshing, Jared admitted silently to himself as he brought his amusement under control. How long had it been since he had enjoyed himself like this? Too long. If he wasn't dashing about from one country to another and working all the hours under the sun, he was attending some social function or other or entertaining at Fotheringham.

And how many of the women he knew would appreciate a walk in the country and lunch in a little out-of-the-way pub? None of them. They liked to see and be seen; image was all-important. There was no amusement on his face now.

And he had purposely gathered people like that about him, people who fitted into his fast— shallow?—lifestyle. The last thought bothered him more than he liked to admit to himself, and his mouth hardened as his eyes narrowed. But that was the way his life was; he had made his bed the way he liked it and he intended to continue lying on it when—and with whom—he liked, he told himself militantly. Nothing had changed. *Nothing.*

He was aware that Henrietta was still staring at him across the table and now he glanced at his watch, his voice cool but pleasant as he said, 'It's nearly two, and I know you didn't want to be too late back. We'd better get moving.'

He was annoyed with her. Henrietta sensed the change in him and her chin rose defiantly in answer to it. Had he expected her to fall at his feet, bowled over by his charm? she asked herself tightly. No doubt there were plenty of women only too ready to do that, but she was *not* one of them.

The walk back was not as amiable as the walk to the pub had been, although outwardly nothing had changed. The day was still sunny and gently redolent of the approaching summer with soft, fresh scents carried on the warm breeze, and Jared's banter was light and entertaining. But he had definitely withdrawn somewhere else.

Henrietta glanced at him as he threw a stick for Murphy, who had deigned to concede to chase it whilst still keeping a watchful eye on his mistress and returning to her side every minute or so.

She didn't want Jared to be all over her anyway, she told herself firmly. It would only have necessitated an embarrassing rebuff on her side, and he was still her landlord when all was said and done. No, far better that he realise himself they had nothing in common and she wasn't his type of woman.

She gave a mental nod of affirmation even as she berated herself for the pang of desolation the thought had produced, and turned her gaze resolutely to the front. Ever since the day she had first met him he had persisted in remaining at the forefront of her mind despite all her efforts to the contrary. And it had to stop. She would *make* it stop.

Once in the car, with Murphy panting as loudly as a steam engine and stinking to high heaven—halfway back he had managed to find the only muddy oasis for miles which he had wallowed in with sheer relish—the atmosphere was easier, if only because Henrietta and Jared were both concentrating on breathing in as much fresh air through the open windows as they could, to combat Murphy's incredible smell.

'I'm sorry about Murphy, but I did warn you.' As they drew up outside David's house, Henrietta turned to Jared apologetically. 'He's a very *doggy* dog.'

'Isn't he!' Jared glanced over his shoulder at Murphy who grinned back at him cheerfully, his long pink tongue hanging out of the side of his mouth and his brown eyes bright with what looked suspiciously like suppressed laughter. 'You didn't fancy a dachshund or a chihuahua, then?'

'Murphy is perfect for me.' She knew he was joking, but her tone was still defensive.

'Yes, he probably is,' Jared acknowledged thoughtfully. 'Determined, somewhat awkward, very much his own dog... Yes, I can see he would appeal.' He opened the driver's door on the last words and, after walking round the bonnet and helping Henrietta to alight, opened one of the rear doors with the command, 'Come on, you foul-smelling beast, out you get.'

Murphy stretched on his blankets, yawned once, and then climbed out of the car with dignified aplomb and without glancing Jared's way. It made Henrietta want to laugh. If Murphy had been human rather than canine, she might well have suspected that Jared Vincent had met his match.

'Thank you for a lovely lunch, Jared, and I hope the rest of your business goes well,' she said hastily after she had taken a firm hold of Murphy's lead. 'No doubt I'll see you around some time on the home shores.'

'No doubt.' He reached out a hand and lifted her face up towards him, kissing her lightly on the lips before stepping back a pace and surveying her with narrowed blue eyes. 'Yes, no doubt,' he added thoughtfully.

She hesitated, feeling slightly nonplussed and very much out of her depth as he continued to stand there without moving, his face unsmiling. 'Goodbye, then.' It was breathless, and not at all the concise, firm way she had wanted to say goodbye.

'Goodbye, Henrietta.'

He still didn't move, and after a weak, tremulous little nod she turned abruptly into David's front garden, almost dragging Murphy with her as she fairly sped across the nine feet of ground and began to fumble with the spare key Sarah had given her.

It seemed to take for ever to fit into the lock but then it turned, and to her eternal gratitude the door swung open and she was over the step and into familiar territory.

He was still standing exactly where she had left him when she glanced out before shutting the door, raising her hand in a final farewell which he acknowledged with a silent inclination of his head.

'Oh, Murphy.' Just before the avalanche of little people from the sitting room hit them, Henrietta looked down into the furry face and sighed despondently. 'This has to be the finish now, doesn't it? He's probably going back to Anastasia anyway.' The black cloud settled a little lower on her head. Anastasia. Lady Anastasia Filmore and Mr Jared Vincent. It even *sounded* right.

CHAPTER SEVEN

HENRIETTA drove back to Herefordshire three days later feeling more unsettled and on edge than she had ever felt in her life. She hadn't heard from Jared since the evening he had dropped her off at David's after their walk, but on the morning of her departure from London David had opened his newspaper at breakfast and given a long, low whistle.

'What do you know?' He had glanced first at his wife and then at Henrietta, both of whom had raised enquiring faces at the note in his voice. 'He gets around a bit, doesn't he?'

'Who?' Sarah asked patiently. She was used to David's irritating habit of asking questions that were unanswerable.

'Jared Vincent.'

Henrietta's heart stopped and then began to pound so hard she felt nauseous. Whatever this was she wasn't going to like it.

'Says here he's just won some business accolade or other for acquiring a heavy contract that keeps the work in England rather than losing it abroad,' David read from the newspaper

164

in front of him. 'Real feather in his cap, apparently, and from what it says here he's got his
financial finger in more pies than little Jack
Horner. He'd got 'em all bowing and scraping
to him at the Savoy last night anyway. Here,
have a look, Hen.'

She didn't really want to look and yet nothing
could have stopped her, although she never did
make much sense of what was written—it was
the picture that took all her attention. There was
a smiling Jared looking straight into the camera
with his own particular brand of arrogance clear
to see, and who was hanging on his arm? Who
else but Lady Anastasia Filmore.

'Who's the blonde, Hen? Do you know her?'
David asked with the tactlessness inherent in all
big brothers.

'I've seen her, that time just before Christmas
when I was invited to Fotheringham,' Henrietta
said dully without raising her eyes from the
beautiful, cool face looking at the camera with
such disdain. 'Her name is Lady Filmore; she's
a friend of his.'

'A friend, eh? Oh, boy...'

David's voice was richly appreciative, but
when Sarah said sharply, '*David*,' with a nod of
her head at Henrietta's white face, he added

somewhat weakly, 'Well, she's obviously pho-
togenic. The camera can be really flattering.'

'No, she really does look as good as that,'
Henrietta said flatly, before raising her head and
looking at the two concerned faces in front of
her as she added, forcing a smile, 'It's okay,
don't look so tragic. We aren't even dating.'

'I *hate* him.' Henrietta spoke out loud, and
Murphy whined enquiringly from his vantage
point on the back seat of the Mini. 'I do.' She
repeated the statement as she tried to convince
herself she meant what she said. 'I hate him.'

Of course she had no justification for her
sense of betrayal or hurt, she told herself harshly
in the next instant. Jared was a free agent—completely, utterly, *absolutely* free—and it had been
her who had refused to get involved, not him.
If he wanted to bed the whole of London he was
perfectly at liberty to do so. In fact if she *had*
been dating him she still wouldn't have had any
recourse—he had made it plain that commitment was not an option. Oh, this was crazy.

She stopped her feverish thoughts along with
the car, and breathed deeply for some moments
in an empty pull-in off the A road she was following. She owed it to Murphy—as well as herself—to concentrate on her driving, and she

ought to be pleased that Jared wasn't overly interested in her, or relieved at least.

He was obviously still playing the field, and who could blame him when he had society beauties like Anastasia Filmore panting at the leash? This served her right actually; she had really been letting her imagination run away with her big time, she told herself severely. Why would a man like Jared—an enormously wealthy, devastatingly attractive and frighteningly powerful man—bother about a little nobody like her for anything more than a fleeting moment?

She had been a momentary change from his usual diet—that was all—and she had obviously not been to his taste. And now it was home to the mill and peace and quiet. The exhibition had given her several definite orders for her pottery and two commissions for very lucrative portraits, and she was going to have her work cut out to keep on schedule. This was an exciting time—a rewarding time—and nothing, and no one, was going to knock her off line.

The light was already beginning to fade when she started the engine again, and an icy, misty drizzle necessitated the use of the windscreen wipers for the last part of the journey. The weather had well and truly broken the day before, and now the cold, wet Saturday evening was more reminiscent of November than April.

Henrietta had planned to leave London that morning, but the children's persuasive power as they had begged her to stay until after lunch had meant it was nearly three o'clock before she had got on her way. But she did so adore her three nieces and nephew. She smiled to herself as she recalled the riotous goodbyes, with Murphy adding his fair share to the general bedlam as he had rolled on his back to have his tummy tickled, and taken it upon himself to wash each small face.

They were great kids, Henrietta thought wistfully. Every time she saw them it confirmed to her she could never have willingly given up any chance of having a baby of her own as Melvyn had wanted. She loved children and animals—they were so uncompromisingly *honest*—although the way her life had turned out motherhood seemed a far-off, distant dream.

As Henrietta approached the unmade road leading down to the mill some time later the rain was coming down in torrents, angry squalls buffeting the little car and causing the windscreen wipers to labour.

It would certainly have made for a more comfortable journey if she had left earlier, Henrietta reflected ruefully as she drove very carefully down the high-hedged lane, the car headlights piercing the murky shadows as they bumped their way homewards. Murphy was sitting very still and silent on the back seat of the Mini without even a pant, as though he knew his mistress needed every little bit of concentration she could muster.

When the lights of the mill came into view Henrietta breathed a long sigh of relief, but in the next instant she spoke out loud as she said, 'Lights? There shouldn't be lights on, Murphy.' And if she wasn't mistaken that was a thin spiral of smoke coming out of the chimney. What was going on?

Jared was going on. As the Mini drew to a halt on the gravel outside the mill the front door flew open, and there he stood in the doorway— big, dark and—from the frown on his face— angry.

He had opened the driver's door before Henrietta had unbuckled her seat belt. 'Are you all right?' he demanded in a low, controlled voice.

'All right?' she echoed stupidly, so taken aback at seeing him she made no attempt to move.

'You've taken the devil of a time to get here,' he bit out sharply. 'I was beginning to think you'd had an accident. Why did you leave London so late? You must have seen the weather forecast and realised driving conditions were going to be bad, and the road to the mill is treacherous. It was sheer stupidity to attempt it in the dark in a grossly unsuitable vehicle.'

She stared at him for a few moments, paralysed by the attack and all the memories it brought scalding to the surface, and then she was out of the car like a shot, her eyes flashing and her face white. 'It's absolutely nothing to do with you when I chose to drive back,' she said furiously. 'I don't have to explain my actions to you or anyone else. And how do you know when I left London anyway?'

'I phoned David's to speak to you just after you'd gone this afternoon.' Jared's voice was cold as the icy drizzle falling on their faces.

'Did you?' She had been through this scenario of accusation and censure before, and there was no way—*no way* she was being told what to do by a man she barely knew, a man who had just *flaunted* one of his other women under her nose, Henrietta thought wildly. Melvyn had criticised and disparaged her until she hadn't known black from white, the mental abuse building up until she had been a step away from a breakdown when he was killed. 'Well, I didn't ask you to phone, did I?' she snapped hotly. 'And if I had decided to come home at midnight it's no business of yours.'

Henrietta was aware she was behaving badly; in fact a tiny part of her that was standing back and watching was horrified, but it was pure self-preservation.

'That's all you can say?' In contrast to her fevered state, Jared was the epitome of cool, dark and dangerous as he turned and walked back into the house, and after a second of blank surprise Henrietta followed with an anxious Murphy hot on her heels. The big dog hadn't liked their angry voices or the crackling air waves, and now a low rumble sounded at the back of his throat.

'I don't *have* to say anything,' Henrietta snapped, her voice tight. 'That's the whole point. And where do you think you are going now?' she added militantly after Jared stared at her for one more moment before continuing through to the kitchen.

'I'm collecting my coat, do you mind?' he asked with controlled sarcasm over his shoulder.

'Yes, I do as it happens,' she shot back. 'I mind very much.'

'Tough.' The blue eyes swung to face her and now his face was grim as he swung his coat over one shoulder and brushed past her into the hall.

Henrietta was so mad she was ready to explode. How dared he think he could tell her what to do, and what gave him the right to be waiting for her here like this anyway? Anyone would think he owned the place. Well, he did own it—the acknowledgement of the fact did nothing to curb her angry frustration—but that didn't mean he could just barge in whenever he liked, and certainly not when she wasn't there. She had taken a three-year lease for goodness' sake; if he wanted to come over the threshold he should ask permission or wait for an invitation like everyone else.

She spoke her thoughts out loud as she followed him back into the hall. 'You might own the mill, Jared, but I've signed an agreement to rent it for the next two years and that means it's my home till then. If you want to enter the premises I'd prefer you to make an appointment in future. All right?'

'Fine,' he snarled furiously. And then, as Murphy's rumble became a fully fledged, gummy growl, he added, 'And you can shut up too,' before slamming the front door behind him.

'Oh…!' The exclamation left Henrietta in a long, shuddering sigh that brought Murphy's wet nose nudging at her hand. 'Oh, Murphy.' She tottered to the bottom step of the stairs and sank down on the varnished wood, the sound of a car from the back of the mill bringing her drooping head up as she listened to the Range Rover's powerful engine. There was a harsh jarring of gears that made her wince, the screech of tyres, and then a roar as the large vehicle drove round and past the mill far too fast.

Silence descended, the beating of the rain and the howling of the wind against the windows the only sounds.

How long Henrietta sat there in a stunned stupor she didn't know, but eventually she roused herself to bring in her suitcase and bags from the car, locking the front door behind her before she walked slowly up the stairs and into the big, oak-beamed sitting room on the second floor.

She stood for a moment looking around. There were fresh flowers in a big vase under the leaded little side window that looked out across the River Arrow to rolling countryside beyond, and a massive pile of chopped logs on the big stone plinth adjacent to the fireplace. The wood-burning stove was roaring away, filling the room with warmth and a cosy glow, and the curtains were drawn to shut out the dark, windy night. The room looked welcoming and snug, and she suddenly wanted to howl as her fear and anger drained away.

She felt even worse after she had unpacked and investigated downstairs. The fridge was stocked with goodies including thick steaks and a couple of bottles of expensive wine, there were fresh eggs and bread on the kitchen table and even a big juicy bone which she assumed was meant for Murphy. How she had missed it all when she had followed Jared into the kitchen for those few moments she didn't know. Well, she did, she acknowledged miserably. She had been too busy ranting and raving to look around.

He had obviously gone out and shopped for her after he had rung David and learnt of her late departure, and she had been completely out of fuel for the stove so he had brought all the logs too. He had warmed the place through, made it nice, and she had...annihilated him. She shut her eyes tightly as her stomach churned and swirled.

Why had she gone for him like that? she asked herself bleakly. She could have explained it was Sarah and the children who had kept her from leaving as early as she had originally planned; she needn't have fired off on all cylinders. He had only been concerned, after all. But she didn't want him to be concerned; she didn't dare *trust* a man being concerned for her. She had thought Melvyn was only being loving and protective of her at first, and before she had known where she was she was bang, slap in the middle of a nightmare. It started with concern and finished with total domination, she reminded herself wretchedly.

She couldn't eat a thing herself although Murphy made short work of the meaty bone, and later she sat for hours in front of the glowing fire as her mind travelled this way and that. But it kept coming back to one definite point, however much she tried to persuade herself differently. She had to go and see him tomorrow and apologise.

Maybe she didn't know what his real motives were for preparing everything for her, and there was still Anastasia Filmore very firmly in the picture—probably other women too, who knew?—but regardless of all that it had been kind of him. She would make it perfectly clear she hadn't changed her mind about not wanting a relationship, she reassured herself firmly, as well as indicating she was going to be very busy over the next few months and wouldn't appreciate visits by anyone, but she couldn't leave things as they were now. Right or wrong, it would prey on her mind.

Why did he have to make everything so complicated all the time? she asked herself irritably as she rose to let Murphy out for a moment before she locked up for the night. She hadn't had a moment's peace since she had met him and it was all his fault. Murphy padded reluctantly out into the cold and rain and shot back sixty seconds later, ready for his biscuit bone and warm basket.

After settling him down Henrietta went upstairs to her bedroom on the top floor, but in spite of her decision her mind was still too troubled for sleep.

At one o'clock she made herself a mug of sweetened warm milk, at three she had cocoa and biscuits, and at half past four she gave up all thought of sleep and sat by the window, wrapped snugly in the quilt from the bed, and watched a tentative dawn banish the night shadows with delicate pink fingers.

She would go to Fotheringham straight after breakfast, and if Jared would see her—which he might not, she acknowledged with a sick flutter in her stomach—get the apology over and done with before the day started. And then that would be that. The slate would be wiped clean, and there would be no need to do more than just pass the time of day if she ever saw him around.

The clouds were scudding across a heavy, pewter-grey sky when Henrietta rang the ornate bell outside the studded front door of Fotheringham Hall, but it was no longer raining. Her heart was thudding when the door began to open, but it was Mrs Patten, Jared's indomitable house-keeper whom Henrietta had met briefly on the night of the party, who peered out at her.

'Good morning, Mrs Patten.' Her voice was croaky, and Henrietta cleared her throat before she continued, 'I wondered if it was possible to see Mr Vincent for a few minutes? It's Henrietta Noake, from the mill?'

'Yes, I remember you, Miss Noake.' Mrs Patten smiled her severe smile and opened the door wider. 'Mr Vincent is having breakfast at the moment but I will tell him you are here. Perhaps you'd like to wait in the morning room?'

'Thank you.' Henrietta was feeling more and more like an errant child. The morning room was as immaculate as the rest of Fotheringham Hall, the heavy blue drapes at the window and dull gold furnishings impressive, but as Henrietta sat down on the very edge of a beau-

tiful velvet sofa, her knees tightly together and
her hands clasped, she shivered. It was partly
due to the temperature—the room was obviously rarely used and chilly—but more to do
with the fresh realisation of just how wealthy
and influential Jared was.

Maybe he would just ask Mrs Patten to take
a message and request that she leave? Henrietta
wriggled a bit and then forced herself to sit still.
Or perhaps he would sweep in, every inch the
feudal lord and master? Whatever, one thing
was for certain. He would still be furious with
her.

And then her thoughts were cut off as the
door opened again and her head shot up. 'Mr
Vincent will see you now, Miss Noake, in the
breakfast room.' There was a note of disapproval in the housekeeper's stiff voice. 'If you
would like to follow me?'

'Thank you.' Henrietta's face was flushed as
she followed the older woman out of the room
and along the magnificent hall to a door on her
right. This felt like an audience with her old
headmaster.

'Miss Noake, Mr Vincent.' And then, as the
housekeeper stood aside for Henrietta to enter,
she added, 'I'll bring another cup and saucer
shortly, Miss Noake.'

'Oh, please, don't worry. I don't want...'
And then her voice faltered to a halt as she
stepped into the room and understood the reason
for the older woman's disapproval.

The breakfast room was smaller than the one
she had just been in, the wood-panelled walls,
big oak table and chairs, deep red carpet and
curtains giving an impression of warmth and
friendliness that had been missing in the more
formal morning room, and this feeling was further enhanced by the roaring coal fire in the
beautiful ornate fireplace.

But Henrietta wasn't noticing the room. All
her attention was fixed on the big dark man sitting in relaxed ease at the table clad only in a
short towelling robe, which was open and hanging loose, and black silk pyjama bottoms.

'Henrietta.' Jared smiled, his voice soft. 'And
what can I do for you?' he asked smoothly. 'Do
come and sit down and tell me.'

She had seen a partially dressed man before—
she had been married, hadn't she? she told herself wildly. A man's body was no mystery to
her. But Jared Vincent was something different.
He was...well, he was just overwhelming, she
acknowledged faintly.

His thickly muscled torso was liberally covered in tight black curls across his chest, his

stomach hard and lean, and he had turned his chair to watch her as she came in so that the full length of his body was visible. The black silk pyjamas accentuated, rather than diminished, the power of the very male thighs and legs, and his feet were bare, increasing the impression of undress.

He had obviously had a shower before coming down to breakfast and his hair was damp, curling on to his forehead in jet-black waves that made him look tousled and very, very sexy. He was dynamite.

'I... I didn't realise—' She took a deep breath, willing herself to take control. He had purposely sent for her to come in here, knowing full well how she would be affected, Henrietta told herself desperately, and she couldn't give him the satisfaction of seeing how shattered she was. But she was. Oh, she was. 'You shouldn't have interrupted your breakfast,' she managed fairly coherently after another silent pull of air. 'I could have waited or come back another time.'

'I'm not interrupting it.' He rose lazily to his feet, pulling out a chair to one side of him as he indicated for her to be seated. 'I would like you to join me.'

'Thank you but I've already eaten,' Henrietta said hastily.

'A coffee, then. Mrs Patten is fetching another cup.'

He continued to stand there and she could do nothing else but walk across and sink into the seat, which was a relief as it happened. Her legs were trembling so much she doubted if she could have stood there much longer anyway.

'Now,' he murmured silkily, once she was sitting stiffly to one side of him and he had resumed his seat. 'What can I do for you, Henrietta?'

She would have surprised Jared and shocked herself if she had answered that truthfully, and instead she said, her voice tight, 'I came to apologise for my behaviour last night. I…I overreacted, I know that, and you had been very kind in filling the fridge and getting the fuel in and so on. I must reimburse you.'

'Don't be silly, Henrietta. I don't want your money,' he said evenly.

'Please, I would prefer to.' She took yet another deep breath, and now she couldn't quite disguise the trembling deep inside as her voice quivered slightly. 'I'd feel better about my rudeness if you let me pay,' she insisted desperately.

'And I would feel worse about invading your privacy.'

'What?'

She stared at him in surprise, and then, as Mrs Patten opened the door and bustled over with an extra cup and saucer, closed her mouth from the gape it had fallen into. Jared thanked his housekeeper and then, once they were alone again, said, 'I had no right to come into your home, whatever my motives. I see that now. At the time I was merely thinking you would arrive back cold and tired, and I wanted to get the place warm and check all was in order for what was obviously going to be a late arrival.'

The beautiful blue eyes were very clear and piercingly direct as he turned his head to look at her. 'I assumed the privileges of a friend and I had no right to,' he said quietly. 'You have never hidden your dislike or your mistrust of me, have you, Henrietta?'

Oh, help, this was worse than she ever could have imagined, Henrietta thought desperately. 'Jared, I said I was sorry,' she said shakily. 'And I am.'

'There's no need; I was the one in the wrong, not you. Now, how do you like your coffee?' he asked, raising his brows.

Any damn way. 'White, one sugar, please.' She tried again. 'I don't dislike you,' she began slowly.

'But you don't trust me,' he interjected sharply, a note of anger apparent for the first time. 'Do you?'

'It's not you, not really.' This was being forced out of her and Henrietta resented it bitterly, but at the same time she acknowledged she owed him an explanation for the night before. 'I suppose...' She hesitated. This was hard, so hard. 'I suppose I'm scared to death of trusting any man,' she said raggedly.

There was a long, long silence, and then Jared said softly, 'Want to tell me about it?'

'No.'

It was immediate and instinctive, and in spite of the tense atmosphere Jared's face relaxed into a smile. 'Well, that was certainly clear enough,' he said drily. 'May I at least ask if it was anything to do with your husband?'

Henrietta gulped deep in her throat. 'Yes, it was.'

'I see.' Don't tell me the fool was unfaithful to her? Jared thought sharply as he poured the coffee. But it was the most likely explanation. And she had gone on being loyal to him, no doubt, performing all her wifely duties, loving

him. He had seen it all before. Love had a nasty
habit of making fools out of the most unlikely
candidates—until they got wise, that was. As he
had.

Henrietta took the coffee with a little nod of
thanks, her face still aflame. What was he thinking? she asked herself silently. All manner of
things, most likely, but the cool, dark face was
giving nothing away. He would be fantastic at
poker.

'So, it would seem that life has dealt the odd
dud card to both of us,' Jared said in the next
instant, and then, as Henrietta couldn't hide a
small smile, demanded, 'What have I said?'

'Nothing,' she said hastily. 'It's just that I was
thinking you would be good at poker and then
you mentioned cards.'

'I'm good at a lot of things, Henrietta.' He
smiled as the colour that had begun to subside
made her cheeks glow again. 'It's just that you
seem intent on denying me the chance to prove
it,' he murmured regretfully. 'But one day…'

One day nothing. Henrietta sat up a little
straighter and took a big gulp of the scalding
hot coffee, willing herself not to betray the aching desire that had her in its grip. What was the
matter with the man anyway? she asked herself
irritably as she put the cup very carefully back

on its saucer. Why couldn't he dress normally for breakfast like everyone else did? She valiantly ignored the fact that more times than not she breakfasted in her night attire. But then there was night attire and night attire…

'Anyway, I just wanted to clear the air and say how sorry I am,' she said dismissively as she began to rise. 'And—'

'Prove it.' He cut across her apology in a voice that was as rich and smooth as thick cream, his eyebrows raised challengingly.

'What?' She stared at him nervously. He didn't mean…?

'Prove it.' Henrietta was standing now and he joined her, the powerful semi-naked body intimidating. 'Let's kiss and make up,' he suggested with a wicked smile.

'Jared, don't be silly,' she managed weakly.

'Just a conciliatory kiss between friends.'

'You aren't my friend.' She was absolutely out of her depth here and he was far, far too close for comfort.

'But I'd like to be.' His voice was warm and soft, and trickled over her taut nerves like perfumed oil.

'Mrs. Patten—'

'Will only come when I ring for her,' he finished silkily.

There seemed to be masses and masses of bare male flesh to Henrietta's fevered gaze, and as she opened her mouth to protest some more Jared kissed her, drawing her into his rigid body with skilful ease as he manipulated her effort to twist away to his own advantage.

His robe was open either side of the solid wall of his chest, and Henrietta found the hands she had placed there to push him away had stilled as her fingers had become entangled with crisp dark body hair. She was trembling at the sensation and they both felt it, but a primitive desire to feel and explore had gripped her, the musky male smell of him all about her as he moulded her closer against the hard planes of his body.

She shifted slightly in his arms, reaching up her hands to the broad, muscled line of his shoulders, and he crushed her deeper into him, the black silk doing nothing to hide his arousal.

His tongue was sensitising the hidden contours of her mouth and she welcomed it with an abandonment that would have shocked her, had she been aware of it. But she was aware of nothing but Jared, the touch and taste and smell of him filling every crevice of her mind and body until she was liquid in his arms.

The tangled hair of his chest rasped against the thin silk of her blouse, tightening and swell-

ing her breasts as every tiny movement gener-
ated its own sweet, drugging pleasure until the
world was all sensation and colour behind her
closed eyelids. And he allowed the kiss to
deepen slowly, moment by moment, touch by
touch, the tremors that were shaking Henrietta's
body finding an echo in himself.

His hands slid down to the small of her back,
moving her hips forward, and she shivered helplessly as she felt every inch of his manhood
against her softness.

She had never felt like this with Melvyn. The
thought was there but the name inspired none
of the usual connotations of doubt and fear and
self-contempt. Instead there was an aching regret for what could have been if he had been
different, and a straining into Jared's body as
she sought deeper and deeper intimacy.

And then they both heard it, the peal of the
front doorbell as it jangled into the oasis of pleasure and brought them up, gasping for air.

Jared swore, just once but very fluently as
Henrietta jerked away from him, her eyes opening wide and her legs so shaky she had to sink
back into the seat she had vacated. 'Who the
hell…?' He raked back his hair with harsh fingers and then looked down at her, his face torn
with a hundred emotions as he said, 'Henrietta,

we have to talk. Whoever this is, whatever they want, you understand that, don't you? I'll get rid of them, okay?'

'Okay.' It was a weak whisper, but she couldn't help it. Her world had been turned upside down and blown inside out. *She loved him.* Why, oh, why hadn't she acknowledged the truth that had been staring her in the face for weeks? she asked herself tremblingly. Or certainly days. Ever since the moment he had confided in her about his childhood and first love. It had touched something fundamental in her, and she should have admitted it to herself then. It might have given her some sort of protection against just this very thing happening, because she knew—at the heart of her—that she was just one of many strings to Jared's bow.

And, as though in confirmation of that bitter truth, Mrs Patten knocked at the door of the breakfast room a moment or two later before opening it and saying, 'Lady Filmore is here, Mr Vincent. I've put her in the morning room.'

Henrietta thought it was a credit to Jared's housekeeper that her voice was so matter-of-fact and devoid of emotion when she must realise the potential awkwardness of the situation, and Jared himself didn't seem too bothered, his voice merely irritated when he said, 'Thank you, Mrs Patten. I'll be along shortly.'

Did he entertain all his ladies semi-naked? Henrietta asked herself with a touch of hysteria. It would seem so. And now, as the door closed behind Mrs Patten's tall, forbidding figure, Henrietta said quickly, 'I'd better be going; you're clearly busy.'

'Don't retreat again,' he said huskily. 'Every time I get anywhere near close you back off, and it's driving me crazy.'

Henrietta took a deep breath and spoke her mind. 'I'm not into harems, Jared,' she said shakily. 'I'm sorry, but that's how it is.'

'Harems?' He stared at her, a deep frown wrinkling his brow.

He was either a superb actor or that was genuine bafflement on his face, but, in view of the visitor in the morning room, Henrietta awarded him an Oscar. 'Yes, harems,' she repeated quietly, her voice stronger now. 'Put it down to weakness or insecurity or anything else you might come up with, but I'm monogamous by nature and I intend to stay that way. Now, hadn't you better see to your other guest?'

'All in good time.' He was staring at her with a very strange expression. 'Let's get this clear. What, exactly, are you saying?'

'I would have thought that was perfectly obvious,' she said tightly. 'I hardly need to spell it out, surely?'

'Humour me.'

And she might have done so if the door hadn't opened at that moment, and a cool, smooth voice purred, 'Jared, darling? The mountain has come to Mohammed as you can see. Oh. Miss Noake, isn't it? I'm so sorry, I had no idea...'

Henrietta stared right back into the cold green eyes looking into hers, and it came to her that Anastasia Filmore had been perfectly aware of her presence in the breakfast room. The confirmation was there in the studied lack of expression on the beautiful face, and the sweet, modulated voice. Anastasia was angry, furious, but she was hiding it superbly well.

'That's all right, I'm just leaving.' Henrietta forced a smile and the lovely mouth smiled back, baring small white teeth as it said, 'Really? How fortunate.'

For whom? Henrietta kept the smile in place through sheer will-power. But that was a silly question; as far as the lovely blonde was concerned there was only one person in her whole universe of any importance—Anastasia Filmore. Or maybe—Henrietta noticed the hungry, smouldering glance the other woman threw at Jared—maybe two.

Anastasia had come fully into the room now, and Henrietta saw she was dressed to kill in a pale cream linen suit that screamed a designer label and elegant high-heeled court shoes of exactly the same shade. Her pale blonde hair was loose and curled attractively round the heart-shaped face in soft waves that fell to her shoulders, and her make-up was immaculate. She looked every inch a Lady of the realm, and ideally suited to grace Jared's arm.

Henrietta, on the other hand, was dressed in black leggings and a pale violet jumper that was one of her favourites but had seen better days, her hair secured in a high, curly ponytail on the top of her head and her face devoid of all but the barest trace of make-up. Her clothes were perfectly suited to a day at her potter's wheel, her no-nonsense hairstyle likewise—but that didn't help much as the frosted green eyes swept over every inch of her in an inspection that was razor-sharp and blatantly contemptuous.

'I would prefer you to stay, Henrietta.' Jared's eyes were hard on her now, his voice cool and even. 'There's more that we need to discuss.'

'I'm sure it will do another day.' If he thought she was going to stay to be *dissected* he could think again, Henrietta thought with painful recognition of the other woman's disdain; besides which in this case three was very definitely a crowd. She walked towards the door as she spoke, passing Anastasia with a cold nod of her head, and turned in the doorway as she added, in a rare moment of wickedness, 'And thank you again for last night, Jared,' her voice soft with meaning.

She just had time to notice Jared's rather surprised face, and the fact that her words registered in Anastasia's eyes with the force of a thunderbolt as the other woman's gaze narrowed and became positively venomous, and then she was in the hall.

'Henrietta?' Jared was right behind her. 'Let me see you out if you insist on going.'

'There's no need.' Henrietta was feeling mortified that she had allowed herself to be provoked in the first place, and even more that she had responded as she had. It was just the way Anastasia had looked at her, she told herself miserably. As though she were something nasty on the bottom of her shoe.

'Of course there is.' His voice was warm and deep, but Henrietta didn't turn round or make any rejoinder as she fairly scuttled across the baronial hall. She just wanted to get home— home to the mill and Murphy and normality. She knew what she was doing when she was forming her pots or painting her pictures, she told herself feverishly; all that was under her control. And she wanted, *needed* to have charge of her life. But when she was around Jared Vincent it all went haywire.

'Henrietta?' His voice was sharper as she struggled to open the front door, and when a muscled arm reached over her and placed a hand on hers as she wrestled with the handle she froze instantly. 'Look at me,' he commanded softly.

She was terribly aware of the tall, slim figure of Anastasia Filmore as she turned slowly to face him, although the hall was quite empty apart from the two of them and the door to the breakfast room was closed. Nevertheless, it caused her voice to be flat as she said, 'I've said what I came to say, Jared, and I'd like to go now.'

He surveyed her for a long moment, his gaze narrowed and intent. 'And what about in there?' he asked quietly with a nod of his head towards the breakfast room. 'Are you telling me that didn't mean anything to you? Is that it?'

'Yes.' Pride had come to the rescue and her face was stiff. 'That's exactly what I'm saying,' she said defiantly.

'I see.' The blue eyes were razor-sharp, boring into her soul.

He looked dark and overwhelmingly attractive as she leant back against the hard wood of the door, his body an inch or so away but not touching her. She wanted him; she wanted him so badly she felt she could die from it, and she was terrified he would sense it. 'So can I go now?' she asked again, her voice tight as she lifted her chin and stared at him bravely.

'Of course,' he said softly, holding her gaze for one more moment before he stepped back a pace. 'You have always been free to go, Henrietta. You know that.'

You have always been free to go...

Henrietta found the phrase was ringing in her ears as she moved to one side and Jared opened the heavy oak door for her, his face impassive. Free to go... Marriage with Melvyn had meant a prison where every thought—every action— was stifled, let alone her personal freedom to come and go as she liked.

Jared had made it clear he was offering independence and non-restraint in any relationship she might have with him, but that was because he had his own reasons for non-involvement and autonomy. What if—and it was a massive if, she knew that, and one hardly worth considering in view of his lifestyle and attraction to, and for, her sex in general—but what if she grew to mean more than just a current bed partner? What then? But what was she thinking like this for anyway? she asked herself silently in the next instant as she stepped outside into the April morning. Loving him as she did, she couldn't bear to be just another notch on his belt; that would be just as horrendous as her relationship with Melvyn had been, but in a different way. Either way anything between them was doomed.

'Goodbye, Henrietta.' It sounded chillingly final.

The hard angles of his face were very defined in the dull, dingy light as she turned to say goodbye. 'Goodbye.' It was a whisper, and she noticed in a little separate part of her brain that it had started to rain again, a thin, persistent drizzle coating her hair and eyelashes as she walked over to her car at one side of the drive. Anastasia's Mercedes was parked just a few feet away, and there was no possibility the other woman could have missed seeing Henrietta's bright blue Mini. She wondered for a moment if Jared would recognise the fact and realise

Anastasia had interrupted them on purpose, but then she shrugged wearily.

It didn't really matter anyway. It was over, not that it had ever begun.

CHAPTER EIGHT

CONTRARY to what Henrietta had expected when she had arrived home heartsore and desperate after her last visit to Fotheringham Hall, the next two weeks whizzed by.

She set herself to work from dawn to dusk on the new orders the exhibition had procured, and as always the pleasure and creative fulfilment Henrietta gained from the craft she loved proved therapeutic, providing a welcome escape from her dark thoughts.

The nights were a different story.

The first one was spent tossing and turning in an agony of self-recrimination and pointless wandering down memory lane, and Henrietta was at work in the studio before it was even light the following morning. The next night proved no better, and so a pattern was set.

Henrietta worked in the studio far into the night, only plodding upstairs to the top of the mill and bed when she was too tired to think, let alone work, and then she would rise as soon as she awoke—usually with the first glow of dawn—and begin the process over again once she had washed and dressed.

Her only break from the potter's wheel was when she took Murphy out for a walk, and even that was done with a dogged, relentless energy that had Murphy flopping down exhausted on their return and sleeping the hours away in canine contentment.

She worked, she shopped and cooked and she walked, and all the time, at the back of her mind, she fought a tall, dark, aggressively handsome giant of a man every inch of the way.

It had helped a little when, on the second morning, Ronald had called in for one of his customary chats and mentioned that Jared had been called away on urgent business for a few days.

'Mind you, he's spent more time here at Fotheringham lately than he's ever done before,' Ronald had commented thoughtfully, before taking a big gulp of his coffee. 'We normally only see him at high days and holidays, you know? The old man, his grandfather, was a great one for getting a finger into every pie that was going, and Jared's the same if not more so.'

Henrietta had nodded noncommittally as she thought of Anastasia Filmore. There was probably a very good reason for Jared to spend more time at Fotheringham, she'd thought waspily, now the beautiful blonde was displaying such an interest in its owner. But the fact that she knew there was no chance of her bumping into him on her walks with Murphy had made the time outside more relaxing.

But then, on Ronald's next visit exactly two weeks later, Henrietta's misery over Jared was pushed temporarily into the background as another, more urgent worry came to the fore—one concerning Murphy.

'I haven't just come for a social chat this time,' Ronald began as soon as she opened the door to him on a beautiful May morning that reeked of wild flowers and sunshine and blue skies. 'It's a little more serious than that, I'm afraid.'

'Serious?' She thought immediately of Jared and her face turned white. 'What is it?' she asked apprehensively.

'Can I come in and explain?' Ronald asked quietly, and then, when she waved him in with a quick, 'Oh, I'm sorry, Ron, of course, come in,' he added, 'It might be something or nothing as it happens, but I'd prefer you to be on the look-out.'

'Oh.' She stared at him nonplussed and then urged him through to the kitchen. 'I'll make a coffee while you tell me.'

'We've had several reported cases of strychnine poisoning in domestic pets,' Ronald said soberly as he sat down at the kitchen table. 'Cats, down in the village. Now, I know all the gamekeepers hereabouts and other people that use strychnine to kill vermin, and they appreciate it's a deadly drug and use it with great care, but either someone's slipped up or...'

'Or?' Henrietta asked him faintly, her eyes widening.

'Or we've got a nutter out there,' Ronald said grimly. 'Someone with a grievance maybe, or just someone who doesn't like cats—or dogs. The big cities haven't got the monopoly on weirdos.'

'Dogs?' Henrietta heard the shrill note in her voice and forced herself to speak quietly. 'You mean he might start on dogs next?' she asked weakly.

'I haven't said this is malicious, Henrietta, so please don't worry too much,' Ronald said firmly, 'but it is a possibility and one you must be aware of. Keep an eye on Murphy when you let him off the lead, don't let him forage or dig anything up and eat it—things like that. Cats are great scavengers, and the ones that died might just have been in the wrong place at the wrong time. It happens in country areas occasionally.'

'What…what are the signs to look for, just in case?' Henrietta asked nervously. 'How would I know?'

'Oh, you'd know if it happened.' Ronald's voice was grim, and then, at her anxious face, he added, 'They go into a spasm—spine arched, head pushing backwards and legs straight and straining.'

'And what could I do to save him?'

'Nothing, Henrietta.' Ronald shook his head slowly. 'The only hope is to get the animal to a vet who would administer apomorphine, but that is rarely successful once the poison is in the system. However, I'm sure Murphy is going to be perfectly all right. The news has got about regarding the cats. If someone has been neglect-ful, which I suspect they have, they'll cover their tracks and dispose of the evidence some-where safe now they know animals are dying. I had to tell you as a precaution, but don't worry.'

But she was worried. She was very worried.

For the next few days after Ronald's visit Henrietta didn't let Murphy off the lead on their walks—something the massive German shep-herd made clear he took as a personal insult—

instead walking miles further than normal as she exercised the big animal. He was used to wandering in and out of the mill while she worked now the good weather had arrived, and when she shut the door to the studio too Murphy sat looking out at the gurgling river and green grassy banks mournfully, whining now and again deep in his throat at the gross unfairness of life.

Two of the cats Ronald had mentioned had lived in isolated cottages halfway between the village and the mill, the rest being from homes situated in the village, and this fact—coupled with the knowledge that if the worst happened and Murphy did eat infected meat she was too far away from the local vet to get help quickly enough—made Henrietta extra careful.

However, after another week had passed and no new cases had been reported she relaxed enough to open the studio door again, although she watched Murphy like a hawk when she let him off the lead on their walks.

And it was on one of their walks a full month after she had last seen Jared that the cantering of a horse's hooves interrupted a quiet sojourn by the river a mile or so from the mill. Henrietta was sitting on a grassy incline under the shade of an old oak tree, watching Murphy splash about in the shallows and scare all the fish, and as she raised her head, shading her eyes from the glare of the sun with her hand, she saw him. Jared. And her heart went haywire.

She was wearing a vivid burnt-orange, ankle-length sundress, and the dash of colour against the green grass and flowing river meant he couldn't help but notice her. He waved—she waved back—and then, as the horse began to trot towards her, she rose slowly to her feet and watched him draw near, her heart beating a wild tattoo as it hammered against her rib cage.

He looked wonderful, *wonderful*. She didn't want to be aware of every little detail about him—she never had been before with any other man, even Melvyn in the first heady days of their courtship—but she didn't seem to be able to help it. He was dressed casually as befitted a ride on horseback on his estate, in dark blue denim jeans and an open-necked shirt of the same material. He looked lean, hard, and—as he got within a few yards of her—distinctly cool and distant, which, taking into account their last parting, was perhaps understandable. Nevertheless it still hurt, and that made her angry with herself—and him.

'Hi.' He didn't smile.

'Hello.' Neither did she.

Ebony pranced a little, his eyes rolling at Murphy who had stopped his splodging about at the water's edge at Jared's approach and moved to within ten or so protective feet of Henrietta. Jared dismounted quickly, reassuring the black stallion with a softly crooning voice as he stroked the velvet muzzle that housed wickedly sharp white teeth, before turning to Henrietta and saying, 'He's nervous.'

He's not the only one. 'I'll send Murphy back into the water; he might settle then,' Henrietta offered hurriedly, glad of the excuse to break contact with those devastating blue laser beams. Why, oh, why had she had to go and fall in love with the most incredible man this side of the moon? she asked herself desperately as she re-assured Murphy all was well and persuaded the big dog back to the river. Why couldn't she have gone ga-ga over a nice, ordinary sort of guy, a nine-to-five sweetheart who was content to mow the lawn on a Sunday and take her out to dinner once a month? A controllable sort of man? First Melvyn, and now Jared. Was she *mad*?

'How are you?' Jared had tied Ebony to a branch of the oak tree and now, as she climbed back up the incline, strolled lazily to her side, flinging himself on the warm grass and patting the space beside him invitingly. 'You look as though you've lost weight,' he observed expressionlessly.

'Do I?' Did that mean he thought she looked slim and alluring, or merely that she was too thin? Henrietta asked herself silently. She considered him for a moment through thick silky lashes before sinking down beside him. 'So do you,' she said honestly.

'Million-dollar deals and living on a knife-edge; you know how it is.' He was laughing at her, she knew it, although the tanned face was perfectly serious, and as she looked at him reprovingly he grinned. 'Actually I've been in the process of letting go of a few strings,' he said evenly, his smile fading. 'I thought I'd like to spend more time in England over the next few years, and that meant delegating responsibility where I'm able to, and I've found I *am* able to fairly widely.'

'Oh, I see.' She nodded inanely as her thoughts immediately focused on a slender, ice-cool blonde. Was Anastasia the reason for this sudden preference for England's green shores? she asked herself miserably, the picture of them in the paper suddenly in the forefront of her mind. She was beautiful, intelligent, wealthy and undeniably genteel; she would be the perfect mistress for Fotheringham.

'Do you remember you once instructed me on the difference between cynicism and awareness?' Jared asked softly as the silence between them stretched and lengthened.

'I didn't exactly instruct you,' Henrietta said defensively, disliking the implication she had preached at him. 'I just gave you my opinion, that's all.'

'Forcibly as I recall.' It was very dry.

'There are some things I feel strongly about.'

'Me too,' he said with deep emphasis. 'Oh, me too. One of which—' He stopped abruptly. 'But I'm going ahead of myself here.'

He was stretched out at the side of her but Henrietta had sat down very demurely, her knees brought up under the concealing folds of her dress and her arms wrapped round her legs. She was sitting very straight and stiff, and she felt straight and stiff. He *always* made her feel straight and stiff, as though she were an old fuddy-duddy who was way, way behind the times—until he kissed her or touched her, that was. And then she was anything but stiff. But she couldn't let that happen again, she told herself firmly. Not if she had an ounce of self-respect. *And she had*. It had been clawed back inch by precious inch, and she didn't intend to lose it.

And then she made the mistake of turning her head and looking down at him, and emotions as chaotic as the swirling river just below them deluged her at the look in his eyes. 'I've missed you.' His voice was very soft and slightly husky. 'More than I would have thought possible.'

No, no, she wasn't going to have this. This wasn't *fair*. 'I'm sure you've had too much to do to miss me.' She had wanted to sound stern and assertive, and she merely sounded breathless.

'Then you're wrong,' he said simply, and then, when she made an agitated movement away from him, his voice roughened and he caught at her arm, his hand relentless. 'And you are going to listen to me, Henrietta, whether you want to or not. It's not just this time I've missed you as it happens,' he went on swiftly, ignoring her quickly drawn-in breath and little gesture of repudiation. 'Ever since the first time I saw you you've remained persistently in my mind, whatever I'm doing, whoever I'm with. I thought it was just physical desire at first, something that would either diminish on further acquaintance or get stronger, in which case I could deal with it by taking you to bed, but it's more than that.'

'I don't believe you.' She jerked away from him sharply.

'I don't blame you,' he said evenly as his hold on her tightened. 'It's taken me some months to accept the way I feel, so I can understand it'll take you a while after all I've said.'

'What about Anastasia?' This was crazy; it couldn't be happening, she thought wildly. And yet wasn't it something she had dreamed of from the first time she had seen him, deep in the secret recesses of her soul? But that had been safe…to dream. She had known it couldn't happen, that Jared wouldn't let it happen, and so to dream had been okay. Now she was being faced with the reality of that dream and it scared her to death. Part of her wanted the dream like nothing she had ever wanted before, and the other part of her wanted Jared Vincent out of her life for good.

Melvyn had told her he wanted her, needed her, that without her life wouldn't be worth living, and she had believed him and married him on the strength of their love. But it had been an illusion, a mirage that had nearly destroyed her and had killed him.

'Anastasia?' Jared's brow wrinkled and then cleared. 'You didn't think…? Anastasia is the daughter of one of my father's old friends, that's all, and the two family firms are tied up in some business concerns and so on.'

'Jared, whatever else I am, I'm not a fool,' Henrietta managed to say fairly calmly. 'I've seen the way she looks at you.'

'I couldn't care less how she looks at me,' Jared said tersely. 'I'm telling you there is nothing between Anastasia and me; there never has been. For crying out loud, Henrietta—' he raked back his hair in that gesture she was beginning to recognise meant intense frustration '—*listen* to me.'

'You escort her to dinners, you're seen with her—'

'I'm seen with a lot of women,' he snapped back angrily, and then, as the expression on her face changed, qualified that with, 'And I don't bed *them* either, before you ask. The last woman I dated was over eighteen months ago, and whatever you may have assumed I am not promiscuous. I've had women—hell, I've told you that already—but I'm not a rutting stallion.'

She winced, but came back with, 'You told me, not so many weeks ago, that commitment could never be an option with you and if nothing else I appreciated the honesty. How come it's changed now?'

'I was fighting what I felt for you and I was lying to us both,' he admitted soberly. 'This is the first time I've ever felt like this, Henrietta; give me a drop of the milk of human kindness and at least try to understand where I'm coming from. I didn't want to fall in love; I didn't want intimacy and commitment and all that goes with it, I admit it. But this feeling has hit me like a ton of bricks and there is nothing I can do about it. It's here, it's staying.'

'You don't know that,' she retorted quickly. 'You've already said those other affairs meant nothing; how do you know this one won't go the same way? You can't be sure of anything, admit it.'

He was as near to losing his temper as he had been for a long time, but only the sure knowledge that he would blow it if he did enabled Jared to take a firm grip on his anger. 'I don't want you for an affair,' he said steadily. 'I want more than that. I've known you for five months and I am sure.'

He had made no attempt to kiss her, and again she admitted her inconsistency to herself as she realised that was exactly what she wanted him to do. And yet if he did she would fight him as never before and keep on fighting him.

She believed him about Anastasia—in fact she believed all he had said, but it didn't make any difference to this gut fear that was paralysing her whole being. It was useless to acknowledge that he had had far more to come to terms with than her, and he'd managed to come through. She could concede the fact in her mind, but in her heart? Her heart was a different story. Perhaps it was because the ordeal she had suffered for thirteen months was still too recent? If she had met Jared five years from now, even two or three, she might have felt differently. But this was now, and it was now that had to be faced. She would destroy them both.

'And I'm sure I don't want a relationship with you of any kind,' Henrietta said stonily. 'I'm sorry, Jared, but that's how it is.'

'I don't believe you.'

She didn't believe how calm he was, and Jared heard his voice with a measure of amazement because inside he was burning up with frustration and fury at the man who had made her so afraid. This wasn't really Henrietta; he knew that deep inside. The real Henrietta who was enclosed within the shell this guy had built round her was brave and resourceful and touchingly valiant. He had seen the real her, time and time again over the last months when she had let her guard slip for just an instant, and he was damned if he was going to give up without a fight.

'Don't judge all men by your husband, Henrietta.' He was dealing in the dark here and he didn't have the faintest idea what card to play but he had nothing to lose as things stood.

'What?'

Her head had been drooping down and now it shot up with a rigidity that told him he was right. This was all about Melvyn.

'Whatever he did he was a fool, or worse,' Jared said grimly. 'I'm not like him and I wouldn't hurt you.'

'You don't understand.' She shook her head despairingly. 'Whatever you're thinking you're wrong.'

'Then explain,' he said sharply, before moderating his voice and repeating, 'Explain. Tell me what you're afraid of.'

'I can't.' How had this all happened so fast? Henrietta asked herself bewilderedly as she glanced at the scenic vista in front of her. One moment it had been just like any other day, the next he had appeared and her world had exploded. And yet the sky was still a deep sap-

phire-blue, the river bank green and dotted with
a million daisies and buttercups, the birds still
twittered at the water's edge... She frowned as
a dart of something pierced the panic Jared's
words had produced. The birds shouldn't be
twittering down there, not with Murphy cavort-
ing. *Murphy.*

'Where's Murphy?' Her stomach turned right
over. *'Murphy!'* And then she shouted again but
there was no sudden appearance round the bend
in the river, and she jumped to her feet, shrug-
ging off Jared's arm with a savagery that told
him something was badly wrong.

'What is it?' He rose with her, looking at her
as though she were deranged. 'He's exploring,
that's all. He'll be back in a minute; it's all part
of being a dog.'

'The strychnine. He can't explore; that's the
one thing he can't do,' Henrietta said frantically.
'Oh, help me, Jared. Find him.'

'Strychnine?'

'Haven't you spoken to Ron?' Henrietta
called Murphy's name again, her voice shrill
and panic-stricken as her eyes searched the
bank.

'I only got back last night and I came straight
round to see you this morning.' Jared swung her

round to face him. 'What's this about strychnine?' he asked softly.

She told him quickly, her words spilling over each other, and as his face grew grim her terror increased.

'Right, keep calling him,' he said quietly. 'I'll leave Ebony here; he'll be more of a hindrance than a help.'

'Where are you going?' She caught hold of his shirt, pulling it out of the waistband of his jeans in her agitation.

'The last I saw of him he was paddling round there—' he pointed to the field beyond where the river curved and disappeared from sight for a mile or two '—so I'll follow down.'

'I'll come with you—'

'No.' He cut off her distraught voice firmly. 'He might well just be enjoying himself exploring like I said, and he'll probably double back across the meadow in a minute or two. If anything, you walk a little way in the opposite direction to me and keep calling; that way we cover more ground. And, Henrietta—' he caught hold of her white face, looking deep into her horror-stricken eyes '—the chances of Murphy finding anything are a million to one. I agree with Ron; if nothing's been reported in the last couple of weeks it means the thing's finished with. Someone made a mistake and they've dealt with it.'

'You don't *know* that.' She was beyond thinking clearly. 'And if they did make a mistake there could still be some stuff lying around, couldn't there? Or something dead that's eaten the strychnine? You know how dogs love disgusting things—'

'Stop it; you're no good to him like this.' He took hold of her forearms and shook her none too gently. 'Do you hear me, Henrietta? Pull yourself together and get calling. He's going to be fine, I promise you. Strychnine can only be obtained from a chemist with a permit and if someone had been deliberately trying to kill domestic pets at least one or two dogs would have been affected. It's not out in the open, I'm sure of it. The cats probably hunted in a barn or outhouse, even a cottage garden or shed of some kind where it had been used to kill vermin.'

It made sense, it made sense. Henrietta forced herself to calm down and listen. But where was he?

'Now, get calling and I'll check back here in a few minutes, okay?' he said evenly. 'And keep your eyes skinned.'

'Okay.' And then he kissed her once hard on the lips—a comforting, reassuring kiss—and waded knee-deep into the river and over to the opposite bank where he took off at a run, calling Murphy's name as he went.

Henrietta heard Ebony snort and paw the ground behind her but she ignored him, turning in the opposite direction to Jared and walking swiftly along the river bank as she alternately shouted and prayed. He had to be all right, he had to be; she couldn't contemplate anything else, she told herself desperately. Murphy wasn't just a dog to her, he was her family, and she owed the big German shepherd so much. It had been him who had brought her out of the abyss of despair after Melvyn's death, his love and affection that had warmed her when she'd felt her heart was frozen, his companionship that had lightened her countenance when she had thought she would never smile again. *Oh, Murphy, Murphy, where are you?* she screamed silently in her head. Don't you dare eat anything, don't you *dare*.

And then she heard Jared calling her name and she knew instantly—although there was no note of panic or alarm—that something was dreadfully wrong.

She ran back along the path at the side of the river, only to stop in relief as Jared turned the corner in the distance with Murphy leaping

about his feet. He was all right. *He was all right.*
But then why was Jared walking so swiftly, and
why that deadpan expression on his face? she
asked herself as she watched the pair of them
come towards her.

'What is it?' she called apprehensively.
'What's wrong?'

Jared was already wading across the fast
flowing river as she spoke and he didn't answer
her until he had reached dry land, and Murphy
was giving her the sort of welcome that suggested he had been away for five days instead
of five minutes.

'Nothing, nothing, except—' Jared paused,
and then said with the sort of calm that hid anx-
iety, 'He was just eating something, that's all.
A dead animal of some kind although there was
hardly anything left when I found him.'

Henrietta looked up from where she was
kneeling with her arms round Murphy's big
furry neck. 'A rat?' she asked weakly, rising to
her feet. People poisoned rats.

'I don't know, but I think—'

Henrietta never did hear what he thought because Murphy chose that particular moment to
vomit quite spectacularly.

'I'm taking him to Mayfield, Henrietta.'
Mayfield was the local vet whose large practice

was situated on the outskirts of the nearest town some twenty miles away. 'Just to be on the safe side.'

'But if he's been sick…?'

'That's good, but in the unlikely event the meat was poisoned vomiting won't be enough,' Jared said calmly, 'and minutes can make all the difference. I'd prefer not to wait around and see if he does have a spasm. I'll get him to Mayfield across the fields; I can be there in a few minutes whereas it'll take much longer by car, and by the time I get there or shortly after we should know if there's any cause for concern.'

'You can't ride Ebony and carry Murphy,' Henrietta said, aghast. 'Ebony will throw you; it's too dangerous.'

'Henrietta…' He took her face in his hands, his touch gentle and his eyes—those eyes that could be as piercing as splintered glass—warm and soft as he said, 'I'm sure he's okay, really, but if the worst has happened we won't know until it's too late if I stay here. We don't have any choice and there is no more time to debate.'

Henrietta didn't for one moment think that Murphy would allow Jared to pick him up—that was her first surprise. The second was the ease with which Jared positioned himself and the big dog on the horse's back as she nervously unhooked the reins from the branch and handed them to Jared.

Her last sight of them was Ebony cantering away across the fields and Jared holding the reins with one hand and Murphy with the other, the German shepherd's big head peering bewilderedly over Jared's shoulder as they went.

Henrietta found she had to sit down very suddenly. She sat for some minutes before she could trust her trembling legs to hold her, and then she staggered home in the direction of the mill as though she were inebriated, her head whirling.

Jared had said he loved her and that Anastasia meant nothing to him, Murphy had eaten something that could have been poisoned and might, at this very minute, be breathing his last; how had her world fallen apart in just a few minutes? she asked herself weakly. She had felt something similar to this when Melvyn had been killed in front of her eyes, the same sense of disbelief and shocked incredulity mixed with panic and terror.

Once at the mill Henrietta stood for a moment in the kitchen, looking at Murphy's basket and bowl and willing herself not to cry. He was going to be fine, he was—Jared was with him. And then she took a deep, gasping breath as she realised what she had just acknowledged, leaning with her arms outstretched and gripping the back of a chair as she shut her eyes and shook her head. No, she didn't want to put all her eggs in any man's basket again; she couldn't go through the scenario of learning to trust and believe in someone only for it all to go wrong. She loved Jared—she really did love him, but it wasn't enough.

She opened her eyes, switching on the coffee maker which she had left ready for her return before sinking down into the old wooden rocking chair in front of the open leaded window and breathing in the fresh-scented air as she gazed at the sunny scene outside. Murphy, Murphy, Murphy... Her heart was reaching out to the big animal, willing him to be all right, at the same time as another part of her was saying, This thing with Jared can't go any further; you know it at the bottom of you so you've got to tell him.

She was drinking her second cup of strong black coffee, her hands still shaking, when the telephone rang, and immediately she heard Jared's deep, husky tones her heart jumped into her mouth. 'Henrietta, he's okay. Jacob Mayfield's seen him himself and he's satisfied that, whatever else, it wasn't strychnine.

Something disgusting for sure—he's just vomited again—but Jacob's happy the time has come and passed when we'd know if it was poison. However, now he's here Jacob's suggesting he keeps him for a few hours to see if the vomiting settles, and you fetch him tonight. Does that sound okay?'

'That's fine.' Her legs were wobbling again. 'Thank you so much, Jared.' She wasn't going to cry, *she wasn't*.

'No problem.' There was a brief hesitation and then he said, 'I'll call in on my way back and just explain in more detail.'

It was the hesitation that did it, making him seem vulnerable and not at all like the Jared Vincent the world knew, and before she could stop herself Henrietta found herself saying, 'I'll make us lunch if you like? Nothing much, just salad and cold chicken and French bread.' He *had* dashed miles on a mercy mission, she told her other self who had immediately challenged the wisdom of inviting him; it was the least she could do in the circumstances.

'Wonderful. I'll ride back to Fotheringham and get Ebony stabled in that case, and drive down. See you in about an hour.'

As soon as Henrietta put the phone down she was kicking herself. 'Stupid, stupid, stupid.' She

was muttering out loud as she wandered back to
the open window and stood gazing out without
seeing anything. That had been really stupid.
She didn't want to get involved with this man,
couldn't, and now he'd think… Well, it was up
to her to make the situation plain. She was
grateful for his help this morning, she was hon-
oured and touched that he was prepared to try
and change the way he felt about life and love
and make some sort of commitment to her, but
it was impossible. End of story.

She drew in a deep, shuddering breath, her
face desolate. She had to act this way; it was
the only thing she could do, so why did she feel
so *horrible*? And she did. When she thought
about his childhood, his father, the things he had
shared with her, she felt so cowardly, so spine-
less, that she couldn't be what he deserved. She
hugged her middle swaying back and forth in
an agony of despair. And how would her rejec-
tion affect him? Would he retreat back into that
old life, become more cynical and hard? Oh, she
couldn't bear it. She shook her head desperately.
But—she stilled, her face becoming stiff and
resolute—none of that made any difference to
what she knew in her heart. She would be no
good for him feeling as she did, and sooner or

later—probably sooner—he would be more miserable with her than without her.

Jared arrived just after midday, and immediately she opened the door her face and her body language told him he had to tread carefully. Whatever was the cause of her own personal demons she wasn't through, and she was like a cat on a hot tin roof.

'Here.' He handed her a bottle of good French wine without touching her. 'I thought we could both do with a glass.'

'Thank you.' Her voice was jerky and her smile brittle. 'I thought we'd eat on the little patio at the back of the studio; I used your picnic table and benches all the time last summer.'

'Did you?' Jared was happy to talk of inconsequential things if it gave her time to relax, and as he followed her into the kitchen he took the wine and the bottle opener she had just fetched out of a drawer from her. 'I'll do that,' he said easily, 'and Murphy sends his love by the way.'

'It seems strange without him.' Henrietta glanced round the kitchen as she forced another smile. 'Especially in here; I always think this room is a bit spooky although it's not too bad in the day.'

'I know what you mean.' Jared smiled back at her, the blue eyes crinkling and his black hair as dark as midnight, and again the force of his own particular brand of devastating masculinity made Henrietta go hot inside. Their glance caught and held for a moment longer than was natural, and as Henrietta wrenched her eyes away, her body jerking nervously, Jared continued evenly, 'My grandfather used to tell me stories of when he was a boy and there was a miller at Friar's Mill. The mill has always been part of the Fotheringham estate, and his father used to bring him and my great-uncle along when he visited. My grandfather said they spent many happy hours playing in and around the mill, watching the water flowing over and turning the big wheel.'

Henrietta had turned to him, her face interested, and now Jared busied himself opening the wine as he continued talking. 'Of course the wheel didn't survive the war, but it did its bit towards victory by being turned into munitions along with park railings and garden fences and other metal which could be managed without. My grandfather said the mill was a rather frightening place when he was young, at least for two little boys, what with the rumblings of the workings which seemed to shake the whole building, the pit where the inner wheel was that you now think of as spooky—' he turned to her as the cork popped and smiled again '—and which he said they always stood back from in case they were drawn in, and the banging of the trap doors as the sacks of corn were hoisted to the hoppers on the top floor.'

Henrietta took a step or two towards him, watching as he poured the wine into two fluted glasses and then accepting one with a nod of thanks as she said, 'I'd have loved to have seen it then.'

Jared nodded. 'Me too.' He was aware he was talking almost in a monotone, his voice soothing, but it was working. She had looked petrified when he had first come in. 'He used to say he remembered the smell most of all, a slightly musty aroma, and there was always a thick covering of corn dust and cobwebs covered in the same white dust. And of course mice; he said the place was full of mice and the odd rat or two, which the miller's cats used to chase right by their feet.'

'Ugh!' She laughed and he smiled back before saying, 'Don't worry, they're all gone, although we do have a bat or two in the roof.'

They carried the food through to the small patio just outside the studio door together, and contrary to all her expectations Henrietta found she was able to eat her lunch and, more than that, enjoy it. Jared was the perfect companion, relaxed, amusing, friendly, and he didn't once refer to their conversation before Murphy went missing either by word or gesture; in fact if Henrietta didn't know better she would have thought she had imagined it all.

After lunch she showed him round the studio and he asked intelligent, informed questions that surprised her. 'I didn't know you knew anything about pottery?' she asked, after he had made a comment appertaining to the best type of clay to use with a particular forming method.

'I don't—or rather I didn't,' he qualified quietly, and then, as her brows rose enquiringly, admitted, 'I've been doing a little research. Someone I love takes pottery very seriously, and I wanted to at least understand what it's all about even if I'm not gifted that way myself.'

She stared at him, unable to think of a single thing to say to defuse what had become an electric moment, and he stared back, his face straight and his big, lean body absolutely still.

'Don't,' she murmured at last, hearing the note of pain in her voice but unable to hide it. 'Please don't, Jared.'

'Why?' The easy, soothing approach had vanished and she knew it had been an act. 'Why, Henrietta? You know there's something between us—hell, it's been there since day one,' he pressed unmercifully, 'and I've told you how I feel.'

'I don't *want* you to feel like that about me.'

'I don't believe that.' He turned her round to fully face him and lifted her chin with one finger, looking deep into her hunted eyes. 'I don't believe that,' he repeated softly, his gentleness in marked contrast to his previous tone. 'You might not feel like I do, not yet, but your eyes tell me what your lips deny. You care about me—how much I'm not sure, but you *do* care about me, Henrietta.'

'No—'

'Yes.' He drew her against him, his arms steady and firm as they enclosed her against his hard frame. 'I don't know what your husband did or didn't do to cause you to be this way, but I'm not him, Henrietta, and you have to see that.'

His tone had deepened, his voice husky with the smoky edge she had noticed more than once when she was in his arms. He was aroused; his voice betrayed it and so did his body. 'I know you're not Melvyn—of course I do,' she said feverishly as she pushed at his chest, 'but that doesn't make any difference.'

'It makes all the difference in the world,' he said firmly.

'No.' She could feel the beat of his heart under her palm, the warmth and intoxicatingly male smell of him enveloping her with a seductively sweet weakness, and she fought it with all her might, her tone suddenly harsh. 'I don't want you, I don't love you—I don't.'

'Who's talking about love?' His mouth was close, a kiss away. 'I can wait for love; I can be patient when I have to be. Just admit there's a chance for us; open up your heart and see the truth that's staring you in the face. Damn it, we'll be friends if you want for as long as you want,' he growled frustratedly, 'but just be honest with yourself.'

And then, as though to prove the ridiculousness of the friends suggestion, he kissed her, a long, sweet, drugged kiss that was all pleasure and pain. And Henrietta, to her shame and self-disgust, kissed him back, straining into him as her arms wound round his neck. Her mouth was hungry against his and fired the 'go' button in both of them, Jared lifting her right off her feet as he ground her against him in an agony of need.

Dimly, in the back of her mind, Henrietta knew that this was a terrible—the worst—mistake, but still her mouth frantically sought his, her breath coming in little sobs and moans and her hands clinging round his neck.

He could feel the soft fullness of her breasts pressing against the hard lines of his chest, the scented warmth of her silky, sun-touched, honey-toned skin driving him crazy as her body curved into his in a manner as old as time. Her hands moved from his shoulders up into the crisp darkness of his hair, pulling his head down with an innocent, almost clumsy urgency that touched him to the core.

Jared hadn't expected this flare of passion, this overwhelming response, and now he was kissing her again and again as his hands moved up and down her body, his touch urging Henrietta on to greater intimacy in this exquisite glowing world of sensation and light behind her closed eyelids.

He was crouched predatorily over her now, his big hard body covering her slim, finely boned frame as he crushed her against him, bruising the soft swell of her breasts with a delicious ache until their tips hardened to rigid peaks beneath him.

She knew she ought to stop; as Jared's hungry mouth sought the warmth of her skin where the straps of her sundress had been pushed aside she knew this madness had to end, but she was in the arms of the man she loved and reason had no sway.

'You see, you see?' His voice was soft and exultant against her mouth. 'We would be good together, Henrietta, and you know it.'

Good? They would be stupendous, *phenomenal*. She caught his words with her lips, little quivers of desire pulsating through every vein as she rubbed sensuously against him like a little cat.

'It will be a new beginning for us both, the past wiped out and just the two of us facing the future together—'

Her sudden jerk out of his arms and her shocked gasp caught Jared completely by surprise. 'Henrietta?' He saw her eyes were wild with what could only be fear, and the rage born of the disappointment he was feeling melted as he took in her face. 'What is it? For crying out loud, you have to tell me,' he urged softly.

Yes, she did. She stared at him from across the few feet of space where she had backed in her panic as she acknowledged it was the only way he would understand. And through the understanding, when he realised how hopeless any relationship between them would be, he would leave her alone.

'All right.' In contrast to her face her voice was dull and flat. 'I'll tell you, but...but not in here.' Her studio was precious, both a work-place and a retreat, and she didn't want to strike the death-knell in there so that in the forthcom-ing days she would visualise the final moments in her sanctuary. 'Outside, at the table.'

Once they were seated again, Jared's eyes in-tent on her white face, Henrietta called on all the courage she possessed and began to speak. She told him it all: the happy home life before her father had died, her concern for her mother in the succeeding years that had meant she had continued to live at home when her friends were all spreading their wings and flying off to uni-versities and colleges further afield, her unad-venturous social life before she had met Melvyn, and her heady, exciting days of court-ship.

'And then we got married.' As a statement it was simple, but the way she said it brought Jared's eyes narrowing into twin beams of blue light.

'And?' he pressed gently. 'What went wrong, Henrietta?'

'My husband turned into someone else.' She shivered in spite of the warm May sunshine, shutting her eyes for an infinitesimal moment and then continuing, 'It started even on our honeymoon. There was a waiter at the hotel—Melvyn said he was ogling me and that I'd encouraged him, but I hadn't even noticed the man. We were on our *honeymoon*, for goodness' sake.'

She swallowed deeply. 'But that was just the beginning. He was obsessed with me; that's the only way I can describe it. He became insanely jealous, torturing himself, torturing me with accusations and threats...' She shook her head slowly. 'He cut me off from all my friends, criticised the way I dressed, the way I did my hair, the amount of make-up I used. He didn't want me to work because it meant I was in contact with people...men. He was always telling me I was too thin, that my work wasn't good enough to show anyone, that I was hopeless in bed—anything to make me rely on him more. He wanted to *consume* me, control every thought, everything I did. And...and it began to work. I became so confused, I began to believe it was all my fault.'

'Didn't you tell anyone?' Jared asked softly, wishing he could have had just two minutes with this tyrant while he was alive. 'Your mother, Sarah, a friend?'

'I tried.' She raised bleak eyes to his. 'But you'd have to have known Melvyn to understand. He was so *nice*, so warm and funny with everyone else, and he loved me. Everyone was always going on about how transparently he loved me—and he did, in his own way,' she finished painfully.

'That was not love, Henrietta.' He forced himself to keep all emotion out of his voice. 'Whatever it was, it was not love. I think you got the nearest to explaining it when you called it obsession.'

'Anyway, I struggled through from week to week and month to month,' Henrietta said dully, 'and then…then he went too far even for me, confused and bewildered as I was. He said he wanted me to have an operation.'

'An operation?' Jared frowned. 'I'm sorry, I don't understand?'

This was the hardest part, the part she didn't know how to say with him looking at her so steadily. Henrietta rose, turning from him and standing with her back to him as she gazed blindly at the rolling fields and deep blue sky beyond the mill.

'He wanted me to be sterilised,' she stated, with agonising matter-of-factness. 'He was always saying that the past didn't exist, that it was just the two of us together and no one else mattered, and his reasoning was that a child would interfere with our unity.'

Jared found himself paralysed by shock for one split second, and then he remembered the words he had muttered just minutes before and groaned deep inside. But when he had said the past was wiped out and they would face the future together he hadn't meant it as this madman—and he *had* been a madman, this husband of hers—had meant it. Damn it all… He wanted to drop his head into his hands and groan out loud but he restrained himself. She must see that—she *had* to see that. But before he could say anything Henrietta spoke again.

'I resisted, of course, and went on resisting. He made the appointment for an initial consultation without me knowing, and when he came home and told me one night we…we had a row. A huge row. He destroyed all my work, my paintings, and there was one of my father that meant so much—'

Her voice broke, but when Jared stood she swung round, her hands upraised, palms facing him. 'No, please, just listen. Please, Jared.'

He nodded silently, his face as white as hers now, and after she had sunk down on to the bench continued to stand as she muttered, her voice very small, 'I was scared; I really thought he was going to hurt me and I ran out of our apartment into the street outside. He caught me up, he was crying...' She gulped several times. 'He was sorry; he...he was always sorry afterwards, and we were walking home when the accident happened.'

Jared nodded slowly. So that was it. What a mess, what a million-dollar mess, and she'd been left at the end of it to pick up the pieces of her life. And she had...to an extent. But only to an extent. *Hell!* He kept his face expressionless by a superhuman effort. What could he say after that?

'Henrietta, the guy was sick, you know that, don't you?' He wanted to go to her, to take her in his arms and hold her more tightly than he'd ever held anyone, but it was the wrong time. 'He needed expert medical help, a psychiatrist.'

'I said that, when I told my mother and David; I said that, but—' she shook her head helplessly '—they all seemed to think I was exaggerating, that we were just having a settling-in period that all newly married couples had.

And Melvyn wouldn't hear of going to a doctor; it was all my fault, you see.'

'What I *see* is that you have been through hell,' he said softly, 'but all men aren't like that, and there are marriages that are made in the other place.' It struck him that if someone had told him six months ago that he would make a statement like that, and mean it, he would have laughed in their face.

'Maybe.'

'No, not maybe, it's a sure fact,' he said evenly.

'Jared, you may be right.' She shook her head again as she added, 'But I can't believe it, not for me at least.'

'I'll make you believe it—'

'No.' Her voice was chilled with the ice of fear as she interrupted him before he could say any more. 'I don't *want* to believe it; I don't want to take that risk. My life is my own again now, and that is precious, more precious than you could ever know. I don't want to take the chance that you would begin to change, to try and own me—'

'But it wouldn't *be* like that.' His voice was too loud, the control was going, and he forced himself to take a breath before he said more calmly, 'It wouldn't be like that; trust me. I'm not like that slimeball, and I love you.'

'Melvyn loved me.' She stared at him, her eyes withdrawn, and he knew he had lost her. 'And I trusted him.'

He could talk until he was blue in the face and it wouldn't make a scrap of difference. He knew it in his head but he couldn't help trying one more time. 'I can understand how you feel, probably better than most, but you're missing one important factor that could make all the difference. You're physically attracted to me and that's a start—a damn good start—' he smiled but there was no answering flicker in her pale face '—but when you grew to love me all this would become very simple.'

'There is no chance that I would feel any differently about you in the future to the way I feel now,' Henrietta said with a firmness that suddenly made him furiously angry.

'The hell there isn't,' he grated tightly. 'I would make you love me, damn it. There are two people in this equation so don't relegate me to some shadowy figure in the background.'

'You don't understand.' Henrietta stood up slowly, her voice very low as she said, 'I do love you. I think I've loved you for ages although I didn't realise it until recently, and I shall continue to feel this way, I know that, but it doesn't make any difference to my decision. I don't want you in my life.'

Henrietta watched the impact her words had on his face with an agony that was all the more painful for having to keep it hidden, but she had to be strong. She had to be. Jared looked as though he had been dealt a body blow in the solar plexus, but if she hesitated now, if she gave in to the dangerous desire to hold out her arms and commit herself to this complicated, simple, fierce, gentle man, she would never know a moment's peace. He was too charismatic, too attractive, too strong, too... Yes, too much like Melvyn, she thought wretchedly.

'So you are sentencing us both to a life of misery?' he asked grimly after a full minute had gone by.

'If that's how you want to put it.' She raised her chin. 'But I prefer to think I'm saving us from that. You'll meet—'

'Don't say it.' His voice was savage and it shocked her. 'Don't say I'll meet someone else, Henrietta, or I won't be responsible for my actions.' He stared at her for one last moment, his eyes angry and his face white, and then he turned to walk down the incline at the edge of the mill that led through tall waving grasses round to the road and the parked Range Rover.

Henrietta watched him go almost numbly, only her trembling legs and thudding heart convincing her it was really happening. He was going, he was really going, and that last look of black fury had told her he wouldn't try again.

She heard the Range Rover start, she saw it pass the mill a moment later and drive up the lane as though the devil himself were at the wheel. And then there was silence—deep, complete silence. Even the birds were still, as though they knew something momentous had just taken place.

He had gone. Henrietta sank down on to the hard, sun-warmed wood, the beautiful sweetly scented day mocking her anguish. He had gone and it was all her own fault.

CHAPTER NINE

MURPHY was ridiculously pleased to see her when Henrietta arrived at the veterinary surgery later that day, and the big animal's boisterous delight went a little way to easing the desolation and hurt that had gripped her as she'd watched the Range Rover drive away. But only a little.

She waited all that evening for a phone call that never came, and the next day—after just a few hours' sleep—she was on tenterhooks, even though she kept telling herself, over and over again, that he wouldn't come. He didn't.

The second day wasn't any easier, or the third, but by the time a week had crawled by Henrietta had resigned herself to the fact that what had never been was over. Which was exactly how she had ordered it. Exactly.

However, she was finding that her heart and her head worked quite independently of each other, and when, in the middle of the second week and having produced no work that was of a suitable standard to show, she decided to go and have a chat with Sarah. She packed an overnight case and Murphy's paraphernalia within ten minutes.

It was the first week of June, and Herefordshire's pretty village gardens were ablaze with flowers for the first part of the journey, although by the time the Mini came within sight and sound of London's concrete jungle the hot weather was making itself felt within the car's narrow confines, and Murphy's frenzied panting at the back of her neck was doing nothing to relieve her discomfort.

Henrietta was sticky and tired by the time she drew up outside David and Sarah's neat semi-detached house, and Murphy wasn't the only one in need of a long, cool drink.

Sarah was waiting for her, and Henrietta felt quite guilty about her sister-in-law's transparent delight at the impromptu visit, but after they had settled themselves in the garden with two long glasses of chilled lime juice it was Sarah who suggested the reason for Henrietta's visit. 'So…' Sarah surveyed her sister-in-law through half-closed eyes. 'What's gone wrong between you and Jared?' she asked matter-of-factly.

'What?' Henrietta looked as taken aback as she felt, and Sarah grinned sympathetically.

'Oh, Hen, it was perfectly obvious how you both felt,' she said evenly. 'A blind man could have seen it.'

'Was it?' Henrietta thought back. 'But I didn't know then, not really,' she protested weakly, 'and Jared certainly didn't.'

'But you both do now?' Sarah prompted carefully.

'Yes, but it doesn't help.'

It occurred to Henrietta that anyone listening to their conversation could be excused for thinking it was in some kind of code, but it was indicative of her life at the moment. Nothing made sense. 'Who got the cold feet?' Sarah asked expressionlessly. And then, as a sudden thought struck her she said, 'You haven't both got them, have you?'

'No, it's me.' Henrietta took a long pull at the iced lime and glanced at Murphy who was lying across her ankles and generating unbearable heat. 'Metaphorically speaking of course.'

'Okay.' Sarah settled herself back in the garden chair and adjusted her sunhat over her eyes. 'Tell Aunty Sarah.'

Henrietta left out the more intimate bits but in essence she did tell, and by the time she had finished Sarah was sitting on the edge of her seat, her pretty face one big frown. 'Oh, Hen.' She sighed loudly. 'I hate to say it, but he's absolutely right and you are one hundred per cent wrong.'

'Don't beat about the bush, Sarah; say what you mean.' Henrietta's voice was very dry. Sarah never pulled any punches.

'Look, I know your married life was miserable, and I can understand you being a bit wary about jumping in with both feet, but he's not asking that, don't you see? He said he'd give you time; what more can the poor guy do?' Sarah asked reasonably.

'I don't want time.' Henrietta's frown was pugnacious.

'Then why are you here?' Sarah eyed her intuitively. 'If you're sure you've made the only decision you can, why are you here discussing it right now?'

'I just needed to talk it through with someone, that's all, and I wanted a break from working; it hasn't been going too well.' That fact was very revealing—Sarah knew how much she normally enjoyed her craft—and Henrietta could have kicked herself as soon as the words were out. 'It's the hot weather,' she added lamely.

'Hmm.' Sarah drained the last of her lime with an air of satisfaction. 'I rest my case. Here, let me fill your glass and then we'll talk some more.'

But by the time Sarah returned from the kitchen Henrietta had decided the subject of Jared was taboo. She loved her sister-in-law dearly, but David had been Sarah's first boyfriend and their ten years of sublimely happy marriage had given her no inkling of what it could be like to be linked to the wrong partner. And she had made her decision. Murphy raised his big head and she stroked the soft fur thoughtfully. There was no get-out clause and she had known it all along, really. She would treat the next couple of days as a much needed break with her family, and then go back with renewed vigour. If it killed her.

Sarah, however, wasn't quite ready to let the matter drop. She fielded the enquiries Henrietta made about the children with scant regard, before saying, 'You and Jared—can I just say one thing more now you've brought it out into the open?'

'You make it sound as though I've been working undercover,' Henrietta objected mildly.

'Well, haven't you?' Sarah returned pertinently. 'Anyway, that's beside the point. The thing is, I think we can both agree that Jared Vincent is not your average, nine-to-five husband material, right? But you aren't like that either, Hen. Right from when I first met you I could see you were different, that you wanted more from life than just a steady job and a nice guy to come home to before you started a family. This creative thing, it's a real part of you, isn't it? A big part?'

'Yes, but what's that got to do with anything?' Henrietta said bewilderedly. 'I don't see what you're getting at.'

'Part of the problem with Melvyn was that you were both artists,' Sarah said firmly. 'I know he was weird about you as well, but it didn't help that you both had the creative, aesthetic urge too. Jared isn't like that. He's got his own career, he flies high enough to satisfy any man, and he'd be quite content for you to do your own thing too and for the pair of you to fit in with each other. He's his own man, Hen. He doesn't need to prove anything to anyone. He's already got the tee-shirt if you like.'

Henrietta stared at Sarah's earnest face. 'You seem to know a lot about it,' she said flatly.

'Not really.' Sarah shrugged but she looked slightly sheepish. 'It's just that your mother had a good chat with him and she likes him, and David thinks he's the best thing since sliced bread.'

'They both thought Melvyn was pretty okay too,' Henrietta reminded her quietly. 'Anyway, I take your point, Sarah, but could we talk about the price of bread or something now?'

'Sure.' Sarah laughed as Henrietta grinned at her, and the two women spent a comfortable afternoon together until David got home.

'Hen.' David paused at the threshold of the kitchen where she and Sarah were supervising the children's tea. 'I had no idea you were coming down. Did Mum ring you, then?'

'Mum?' Henrietta wrinkled her smooth brow. 'No. Should she have?' she asked in surprise.

'No, no, not at all.' David suddenly looked distinctly uncomfortable. 'In fact we agreed she wouldn't. Well, we didn't exactly agree not to, of course; it wasn't like that. It wasn't necessary to *agree* anything. We just thought it would be better…'

'David, what *are* you talking about?' Henrietta asked patiently after she had watched her brother digging a deeper hole for himself every second. 'I gather there is something I should know—or not know?' she added meaningfully, glancing at Sarah and then back to him.

'No. Yes. I mean—'

'I think you have just blown it, David.' Sarah's voice was struggling not to betray the amusement that had her in its grip. 'And it's no big secret after all; you'll get Hen worried at this rate. Tell her for goodness' sake and put us all out of our misery.'

'Tell me what?' Henrietta demanded.

'It's only about a commission that has been offered,' David said carefully, 'that's all. But it's a biggie, Hen, and if you can pull it off—' His voice was rising with excitement and he visibly restrained himself. 'Well, you'd never look back,' he finished weakly.

'Yes?' So what was the mystery?

'Visage—you know the new health club and hydro that everyone is talking about, the one that costs you an arm and a leg to put your nose in the door and is strictly for the millionaire-plus types?' David said eagerly. 'Well, they want you to do a living sculpture, Hen. We had a confirmation of the offer yesterday and they are prepared to pay for the right person, and they think that's you.' He mentioned an amount of money that nearly made Henrietta fall off her stool.

'What is it? Could I do it?' she asked faintly, hardly able to believe her ears. She knew of a hundred other young hopefuls on the bottom rung of the ladder who would bite off someone's hand for a commission with this sort of prestige.

'No problem.' David grinned at her enthusiastically. 'They want a waterfall effect in the reception area, a fashion cascade of vessels with water falling from one to the other. Obviously the height differential will need looking at, and the back two or three will be on granite pillars with the whole standing on a big plinth—you get the idea? They want an illusion of time, with some of the vessels appearing to be broken and others lying on their sides, that sort of thing. And there has to be an allowance for a small pool somewhere, with natural oils and essences perfuming the air to give an ambience of well-being.'

'Oh, David.' She stared at him excitedly. *'David.'*

'Most of the preparatory work could be done at the mill; you'd only need to be in London now and again,' David continued, 'and they are happy for you to start work in a few months when you've cleared your present obligations. But just think of the publicity, Hen.'

She stared at her brother as a thought hit. 'So why the big mystery?' she asked slowly. 'What else is there you aren't telling me? There's more, isn't there?'

'Nothing that's really specific to the commission; at least—'

'*David.*' Sarah's voice was of a tone that brooked no argument. 'Tell her.'

'It's nothing, not really, but when I was negotiating this it was to be kept under wraps until the offer was definite, and then he would still have preferred you not to know. Mum and I disagree on this; she thought you should be told and I feel if he doesn't want to broadcast his part in it that's fair enough.'

'*David.*' Henrietta couldn't stand it. 'Who are we discussing?'

'It's Jared Vincent.'

'What is?' Henrietta stared at him blankly.

'Jared's the guy who put your name forward to the directors; he's on the board of the Visage group. You know they do leisure centres and women's retreats up and down the country, and—'

'I know what they do, David,' Henrietta said numbly.

'He thought if you knew he'd been involved you'd think you didn't get it on merit, and he assures us you did. He merely brought you to the board's notice, and they investigated and liked your work and were prepared to make an offer to me as your agent.'

'But they would never have known about me if it wasn't for him,' Henrietta said slowly. 'Would they? And if he hadn't been my advocate there is no way a group like Visage would have taken a chance on a relative unknown; they'd have gone for one of the big boys.'

'Possibly.' David shrugged. 'But everyone has to get a break some time to become one of the big boys, and this is yours, Hen.'

Through Jared. *Jared.* Who hadn't wanted her to know he was involved, who had believed in her work enough to put his money where his mouth was. 'You say you had confirmation of the offer yesterday?' she asked quietly as her heart began to pound so hard it was a physical pain.

'Yep. The board met the day before for the final say-so.' David was looking at her strangely now and she couldn't blame him. He clearly expected her to jump and shout for joy, and here she was frozen to the spot. Two days ago. The decision had been made two days ago, so Jared could easily have put the proverbial boot in at any time over the last ten days since their cataclysmic parting. But he hadn't—*he hadn't*.

'I see.' She needed to say something, to at least try and act normally, but it was beyond her and it was only little Amy surreptitiously slipping Murphy a slice of bread and Marmite under the table and falling off her chair in the process that saved her.

But later that night, as she lay in the muggy warmth of the little boxroom with only the faintest breeze from the open window wafting into the room, Henrietta went over and over the conversations with Sarah and David until her head was pounding.

It had been good of him—wonderful—to do this for her and she appreciated it more than he would ever know, but… Had it been a means to an end? Had he known that, people being people, she would get to know of his part in it all? And had he surmised that the knowledge would persuade her into his bed? Oh, she believed him when he said he wanted her, even that he loved her—it was the *nature* of the love she distrusted.

252 THE MARRIAGE QUEST

And she did, she still did, however bleak life was without him and however many tears she cried.

And life was bleak. The sky was less blue, the little things that normally held such charm—the scent of the roses from the trellis under her window, Murphy's lopsided grin, the children's laughter—didn't touch her in the same way, and she felt so *lonely*. So gut-wrenchingly, desperately lonely.

But it wasn't bad enough to risk stepping into the nightmare again. She shut her eyes tight and breathed in and out slowly as the old panic reared its head. If she hadn't been so violently attracted to him at the beginning, and if she didn't love him now, she might have put a tentative toe into the water, she acknowledged silently. But the feeling she had for him already gave him more power over her than he would ever know, and it was for that reason she had to be strong. It would get better; this misery *would* get better...in time.

But she would write to Jared—or telephone—to say thank you. She wouldn't go to see him, she wasn't *that* strong, but she had to express her thanks personally—she owed him that at least.

Henrietta lay resting quietly once the decision was made, the exhaustion seeping out of her in great waves. Awful though this was, she had no other choice, and feeling as she did it was the best thing for Jared as well as herself. She couldn't weaken, not now.

Within ten minutes she was fast asleep.

It was just after two in the afternoon the next day when Henrietta walked into the gallery, arm in arm with her mother and David after the three of them had gone out for a celebratory lunch.

For a moment they didn't notice the tall, dark man standing to one side of the far window and half hidden by a voluptuous giant fern, not until Jasmine—David's assistant—said, 'Oh, Mr Noake, this gentlemen has been waiting for you for a few minutes.'

They all turned and Henrietta watched her mother and brother continue forward, their greeting a mite fulsome, as she remained rooted to the spot. She was conscious of a moment's sharp relief—ridiculous in the circumstances—that she was looking her best in the smart but very feminine white broderie anglaise dress and short-sleeved jacket she had bought that morning, before Jared said coolly, his eyes sweeping over the heads of her mother and David, 'Hello, Henrietta.'

'Hello.' He hadn't known she was in London; she could read it in the shatteringly blue eyes before he turned his gaze to the other two, but he was handling the situation far better than she was, Henrietta thought shakily as she observed his imperturbable countenance and polite, reserved voice as he responded to the gushing torrent of words from her mother. And he looked gorgeous. Tired—there were dark shadows under his eyes—but gorgeous.

Henrietta made the biggest effort of her life and pulled herself together sufficiently to cross the endless space between them, speaking quickly when her mother stopped to take a breath. 'I want to thank you, Jared,' she said jerkily, 'for putting me forward to the board of Visage. It's…it's a wonderful opportunity.'

'My pleasure.' His voice was deep and soft, and she quivered inside. 'You know, then?' he asked quietly, glancing from her to David with a lift of his eyebrows.

'I'm sorry, it was my fault,' David admitted awkwardly, his face flushing. 'I'm not very good at subterfuge.'

'No matter,' Jared said calmly. 'It's quite a refreshing attribute and one I don't often come into contact with in the cut and thrust of business. Now, I was passing and I called in on the off chance. There are one or two points I'd like to go over if you've the time?' he said directly to David.

'Of course, of course.' David was nearly falling over himself in his eagerness. 'Come through to the office. Would you like a coffee?' he asked with a flick of his fingers at Jasmine.

'Please.' Jared smiled at the young girl, adding, 'Black, please,' before turning to Henrietta and her mother with a polite inclination of his head. 'Good afternoon, Mrs Noake,' he said easily, and then, 'Nice to have seen you again, Henrietta.'

He was walking away from her; he was *leaving*. Henrietta couldn't believe or understand the emotions that were coursing through her, and her voice was too loud when she said, 'Don't you want me to sit in on this? Surely you need to sort things out with me if I'm doing the work?'

The two men turned round—David's face clearly horrified at her tone and Jared's inscrutable—and then Jared looked straight at her, his eyes unreadable and his voice cool as he said, 'No, I don't need to sort anything out with you, Henrietta. I know exactly where I stand.' He allowed a pause before adding, his voice smooth now, 'This discussion is purely regarding the economics of the commission; it in no way relates to anything creative.'

'Oh... Yes, of course. I'm sorry...'

Henrietta felt smaller than an atom, and her face must have reflected this because his own relaxed slightly, a slight curve twisting his lips as he said, 'Not at all. Artists have a right to be protective of their best interests, but rest assured that apart from the basic requirement the sculpture will be as you see fit. I will make sure of that.'

He nodded once more before turning abruptly, but not before she had seen a flash of something dark and intense as the sapphire eyes moved hungrily over her face for one heart-stopping moment. She stood quite still as the two men disappeared out of the room into the corridor beyond, her heart racing like a frightened bird's and her head swimming with the impact of that glance. For a moment she felt the way she imagined a small animal must feel when the steel jaws of a trap closed around its flesh and it knew it was caught and helpless.

But she wasn't helpless. She drew herself up, willing her limbs not to shake. And she hadn't been caught either, just the opposite in fact. Jared had made it perfectly clear today that he had accepted her severance of any connection between them. He hadn't prolonged their conversation, he hadn't suggested their meeting after his discussion with David; in fact—she caught her thoughts abruptly, angry with the inconsistency that was making her feel piqued when she ought to be relieved—he had pre-empted their goodbye.

She bit tightly on her lower lip, her hands clenching into tight fists before she realised her mother was staring at her with a very strange expression on her face. 'Is anything wrong, darling?' Sandra Noake asked uncertainly. 'You aren't feeling unwell?'

'I'm fine.' Henrietta couldn't quite manage a smile but she forced a movement of her lips that was a poor apology of the same. 'And I must go,' she added a trifle wildly. 'I promised Sarah I'd pick up some shopping for the children's tea to save her having to bother.'

'All right, dear.' Sandra Noake's voice was neutral but her eyes were very perceptive. 'You run along.'

There was a certain intonation on the word 'run', but Henrietta was prepared to take her mother's words at face value as she backed hastily to the door with a fleeting smile of farewell. She who turned tail and ran away lived to fight another day, she thought ruefully to herself as she hurried along in the warm June sunshine towards the parking meter and her dozing Mini. And Jared Vincent was too formidable an enemy to mess with.

Henrietta found the afternoon passed very slowly in spite of the inevitable bedlam once her nieces and nephew were home—the mayhem ably abetted by a certain large furry animal who entered into the children's games with gusto. She didn't acknowledge the reason for her tense restlessness until David arrived back—alone, and then her misery was compounded by David's cheerful announcement that he had invited Jared to come home with him for dinner— 'I thought it would be nice to have a repeat of that other evening in April; do you remember,

Hen?'—but that Jared had refused, pleading a prior engagement.

'Prior engagement'. The two words haunted her all through the children's teatime and subsequent baths, and she found she was in danger of talking gobbledegook in the midst of Sarah's delicious dinner when she suddenly realised she hadn't registered one single word since they had sat down to eat.

What did prior engagement mean exactly? she asked herself with masochistic bluntness. A business dinner with a male colleague? A business dinner with a *female* colleague, perhaps? A night out with friends, an evening at the opera or theatre with a group of like-minded individuals, or—and here her stomach turned over, and a sickening sense of helplessness enveloped her—an intimate rendezvous for two in some wickedly expensive, discreetly cosy restaurant that was all dim lighting and take-me-to-bed mode?

Oh, she had to stop thinking like this. She found herself glaring at the chocolate soufflé that Sarah had taken such pains with as though it was going to jump up and bite her, and quickly schooled her features into a more acceptable expression. She had no right to object if Jared took a hundred women to bed, none at all. She had made *her* bed and she had to lie on it—alone.

Henrietta went back to Herefordshire the next day, and threw herself into her work with a dogged single-mindedness that meant she was accomplishing three days' work in one. She rose at first light and worked way into the night, barely taking time to eat or drink, and even her normally relaxing walks with Murphy became part of a programme that was punishing.

It wasn't surprising that midway into August and in a heatwave that was blinding she fell foul of a dreaded summer flu that had swept across the country with devastating ruthlessness. She merely felt achy and slightly off colour at first, but by the second day, when Ronald called by on one of his what had become almost daily visits, getting to the front door was a major feat.

'You look awful.' Ronald stared at her worriedly.

Encouragement it wasn't, but Henrietta felt too ill to care. 'It's just a cold.' She stared at Ronald through pink-rimmed eyes, her head pounding as a hundred little men with sledgehammers took aim at her brain. 'I'm going to take a couple of aspirin and rest this afternoon.'

'Have you called the doctor?' he asked anxiously.

'For a cold? No, of course not.' She was feeling helplessly dizzy and her legs had developed the consistency of melted jelly. 'I've told you, I shall take it easy today and I'll be fine in a day or two. You know what these summer colds are like.'

She cut short the normal pleasantries after just a minute or two and, once Ronald had departed, stumbled upstairs to the sitting room where she collapsed on the sofa and shut her eyes. She must have slept, because when she next opened her eyes the room was filled with evening shadows and Murphy was licking her face anxiously, whining deep in his throat.

'Good boy, good boy.' If she had ever felt as ill as this she couldn't remember it, but Murphy needed to be let out and then fed so she had to make the effort to move. She raised her head, fighting back the nausea that immediately swamped her, and, gritting her teeth, swung her legs over the side of the sofa. The room swam and dipped in a crazy kaleidoscope of splintered colour and shapes, and she sank back for a minute or two until the dizziness subsided enough for her to stand.

It wasn't a good idea. Her legs felt like jelly and a rushing in her ears told her she was a second from passing out. She sank down on to the floor as instinct told her it was better to be horizontal, and, after lying limply for another couple of minutes—during which time Murphy washed her face, whining all the time and nudging her with his wet nose—began to crawl towards the stairs.

She bumped down on her bottom, every movement jarring her aching head and sending arrows shooting through her brain. If she could just see to Murphy she could go to bed and she would feel better in the morning, she told herself doggedly. Summer viruses passed as quickly as they came. But she found, once she reached the bottom step, that all she could do was to sit for long moments.

And then the doorbell rang. Murphy's barking inspired the little men into a frenzy, and as Henrietta groped along the wall and found the latch on the door all she wanted was for the noise to stop. It could be a mad axe-man out there, but she really didn't care, she thought helplessly as she opened the door.

'Henrietta?'

She fell into Jared's arms, her voice a low wail as she cried, 'I feel awful, really awful. Could you see to Murphy?' She hung limply on his chest. She didn't question why or how he was here—he *was* here, and that was enough.

'For crying out loud, woman, why didn't you call me?' He was muttering into her hair as he whisked her up into his arms and carried her back into the mill, kicking the door shut behind him and cursing Murphy who was leaping around them like a frantic jack-in-the-box.

Henrietta was aware they were going up the stairs through the pounding in her head, but it was so *good* to be able to collapse completely that she didn't open her eyes until she felt herself placed very gently on the sofa she had vacated minutes earlier, whereupon she forced her heavy eyelids open to see Jared kneeling at her side, his face a picture of concern.

'It's all right; everything is going to be all right,' he said soothingly. 'Just shut your eyes.'

'Murphy... Murphy hasn't been fed,' she whispered weakly. 'If you could just see to him for me? The dog food is in the cupboard by the fridge and—'

'I'll find it, don't worry.'

Her teeth were chattering but she wasn't cold, she thought in surprise as the heat in her body became unbearable. And she was thirsty, so, so thirsty. She forced herself to concentrate on the essentials and added, 'And Murphy hasn't been out since morning.'

'I said shut your eyes, Henrietta.' His voice carried a mixture of tender exasperation and worry. 'I'm quite capable of seeing to a dog, even one as formidable as Murphy.' And then, as she let herself fall back against the pillows and relax, he added, 'How on earth did you think you were going to be able to cope like this? This flu had decimated half the workforce of England in the last few weeks; you can't fight it, woman.'

The flu? She had the flu? Henrietta thought groggily. No wonder she felt so awful. 'How…how did you know I was ill?' she mumbled feebly.

'Ronald,' Jared said briefly. 'Now I'll take care of Murphy and get you a drink and we'll go from there.'

Henrietta awoke a few minutes later to the feel of a firm, cool hand on her brow and the realisation that the blinding headache was worse. 'Right, I've had enough of this.' The piercing blue gaze was too much to handle and she shut her eyes again, too weak to remonstrate when he said, 'You're coming home with me where Mrs Patten can look after you and I can keep an eye on you.'

'But Murphy—'

'Love me, love my dog?' he queried softly. 'Murphy comes too of course.'

She couldn't go, even though it would be heaven. 'I can't—'

'Henrietta, I'm not arguing with you,' he said grimly. 'You are coming home to Fotheringham and I'm calling my doctor to check you out. Then you stay as long as it is necessary, got it?'

She'd got it and she felt too ill to care as she lay on the sofa, aware of some activity and commotion back and forth before Jared was back at her side, wrapping her in a thin car rug.

'I…I can walk.'

'Don't be ridiculous.' He lifted her as easily as if she were a child. 'Murphy's waiting in the Range Rover and I've packed a few things for you as well as his stuff. If there's anything vital I've forgotten I'll come back later.'

By the time Henrietta was installed in a big comfortable bed in one of the guest rooms at Fotheringham she wasn't aware of much except her throat felt as though it was on fire, and the headache showed no signs of abating.

Mrs Patten fussed over her as though she were a two-year-old child—but it was nice—and insisted on Henrietta swallowing a mug of hot lemon and honey along with a couple of aspirin. The doctor arrived some time later, did all the normal doctor things with a professional flourish and then announced she had the flu. 'You'll feel worse before you feel better,' he said cheerfully, 'but a week in bed should do it. Plenty of liquids, don't worry about eating, and keep up with the aspirin and hot lemon. You couldn't have a better nurse than Mrs Patten.'

Henrietta stared at him through bleary eyes and managed a grimace that was meant to be a smile before she drifted off into that other hazy, achily painful world. She continued to skim in and out of it for the next three days and nights, aware of hushed, decorous visits at the bedside by Jared and Murphy, and also the ever faithful Mrs Patten forcing hot lemon and aspirins down her throat at regular intervals, and helping her into the *en suite* bathroom when it was necessary.

The doctor called again at some point during that time, but apart from a splintered conversation in which words like 'obviously run-down before so it's hit her all the harder' and 'mustn't worry, young and strong' came to her ears Henrietta didn't register much.

And then, on the morning of her fourth day at Fotheringham, she awoke feeling she was back in the real world again. The aches and pains were still there, she felt as weak as a kitten and utterly lifeless, but the terrible headache was gone along with the acute dizziness and feeling of nausea.

She lay quite still in the vast bed for an hour or more, watching the sun lighten the room through the closed curtains and just revelling in the feeling of being free from the weird hallucinations that had tormented her in the last few days. She didn't think, she was just content to be, and she was still in that state of peaceful euphoria when Mrs Patten bustled into the room just after seven o'clock with a cup of tea.

'Oh, this is good, you're looking better.' The housekeeper beamed at her. 'Peaky still, but definitely better.'

'I'm sorry.' Henrietta struggled to sit up, finding she was even weaker than she had thought. 'I've caused you so much work.'

'Go on with you, a little thing like you?' Mrs Patten smiled as she handed her the tea after fluffing up the pillows behind Henrietta's back. 'I'm just glad you're feeling better, dear. Poor Mr Vincent has been out of his mind with worry.'

'Has he?' The full enormity of the situation she was in suddenly swept over Henrietta, washing away the serene tranquillity her mind and body had taken refuge in as though it had never been.

'Been overdoing it, haven't you?' There was a tut-tutting from a motherly tongue. 'Now, I've nothing against a woman having a career—I've two sisters and one is a doctor and the other a legal secretary, and two finer women you never met—but it can't be at the expense of your health. You've got to pace yourself, dear. All work and no play...'

'Results in you finding yourself in my bed.' The deep, throaty voice from the doorway brought both women's eyes swinging to Jared and he smiled easily, the bright blue eyes devilish as he took in Henrietta's flushed cheeks. 'Do I take it you're on the mend?' he asked softly as he walked fully into the room, looking the picture of virile health from the top of his black head to the bottom of his feet.

Henrietta was suddenly acutely aware of several things in quick succession, the first—and easily the most disturbing—being that she must resemble something the cat wouldn't deign to drag in, and the second—which was a good runner-up—being that Jared looked even more devastating than usual. Murphy was the third consideration, and as such a safe topic, 'I'm much better, thank you,' she said shakily. 'Where's Murphy?'

'Eating me out of house and home in the kitchen.'

'Oh. And he's been good?' Jared walked over to the side of the bed to stand looking down at her with a strange look on his hard, attractive face, and the shivering deep inside made Henrietta's voice wobbly.

'The perfect gentleman,' Jared said softly as Mrs Patten left the room, closing the door quietly behind her.

'I'm sorry I've been such trouble.'

'Oh, you have,' he agreed gravely. 'I was due to fly out to the States a couple of days ago and you've lost me a very lucrative deal. A small fortune in fact.' He didn't sound too put out.

Henrietta stared at him and the teacup rattled slightly in its saucer. She wanted to say a whole host of things, not least that she was sorry about the lost deal, but words failed her. As the atmosphere became electric she swallowed twice, put the cup and saucer down on the bedside cabinet, and glanced around the beautiful but somewhat flowery room. 'This isn't really your bed, is it?' she asked faintly. She couldn't picture Jared against pink daisies.

'One of them.' He grinned wickedly. 'Actually I'm another floor up; this is one of the guest bedrooms and meant less legwork for Mrs Patten than my room. But the temptation to take you there was strong; I might as well admit it.' And then his voice lost its teasing note as he said, 'Why didn't you call someone, Henrietta— anyone? What possessed you to try and muddle through when you felt so ill? Have you got a death-wish or something?'

'Of course not,' Henrietta said weakly. 'I just thought it was a summer cold, that's all.'

He shook his head slowly. 'I don't altogether believe that. I don't know if it's just that the rest of the world disappears when you're working or whether it's that you don't care about yourself; either way you need someone to look after you.'

'I do not.' She stared at him angrily. He was making her out to be a half-wit. 'And I can leave today now I'm feeling better.'

'You see?' He shook his head again, his voice reproachful and of a tone one would use with a recalcitrant child. It had the effect on Henrietta of making her want to stick out her tongue at him and she resisted it with all her might, instead forcing a glance of regal disdain as he added, 'Nutty as a fruitcake.'

'Jared—'

He caught his name on her lips, his mouth hungry and possessive in the brief moment that he held her, and then he straightened again, leaving her flushed and breathless as he smiled before walking to the door. 'You're not leaving here until *I* think you're well enough; get that into your head first of all,' he said coolly as he turned at the door to survey her through narrowed eyes. 'And we're setting up some kind of ground rules before you go,' he added silkily. 'That's the second thing.'

'Ground rules?' She stared at him in surprise, more shaken than she wanted to admit by the brief embrace.

'Ground rules.' His voice was a relaxed drawl, his eyes on her pink cheeks and tangled hair. 'I was going to give you time, Henrietta, before this latest escapade of yours.' He made it sound as though catching the flu was a capricious whim and her stare turned into a glare. 'Time to get used to the fact that I love you,' he continued evenly, 'and that my love does not mean I want to take you over and control every little part of your life. I love *you*—your strength, your creative talent, everything—and I wouldn't try to alter or deny any part of you. There will be times when you do things independently of me, and that's fine, just fine, but I'll be there, in the background,' he added quietly. 'In case you need me.'

'I don't know what you're talking about—'

'You're my woman, Henrietta.' His voice was husky now, deep and low, and she found herself trembling in answer to it. 'Whether you accept it or not, it's a fact. Now, it might take months, it might take years, but you'll recognize it one day—like I did—because this is not an accident, this feeling between us. It's destined— as inevitable as the rising of the sun and the rhythm of the tides. You're mine, I'm yours, and whatever hang-ups you still need to work through it won't alter that.'

She didn't move—she couldn't; she just continued to watch him with wide, troubled eyes.

'Do you think I didn't feel like you?' he asked softly. 'Out of my depth, *terrified* at the power I was giving to someone else? It nearly sent me crazy, I'm telling you—I thought I was going nuts there for a while; but then I realised it's a process we'll work through together. *Together*,' he added deeply. 'That's what love is all about. I'm not going to give up, Henrietta, not ever.' He eyed her steadily. 'Not because I want to own you or control you or make you into some sort of zombie freak, but because I love you, that's all. And part of that love means I want to take care of you, protect you, and I'm not going to apologise for that. And in time you'll trust me and it'll become easy.'

'What if it doesn't?' she whispered brokenly.

'It will.' His eyes stroked her face tenderly. 'You'll get there; I have faith in you, and I can wait until you're ready. Not patiently,' he added sombrely, 'I'm not built that way, but I can wait. There's too much hanging on this—the rest of our lives, children—hell, grandchildren—for me to do anything else.'

She stared at him, her eyes wretched. 'No, Jared.'

'Yes, Jared,' he whispered mockingly. 'But I'm not being kept on the perimeter of your life any more so you might as well face that little fact right now. And if you run I shall follow you and bring you back, and I make no apology for that either. I'm not Melvyn, Henrietta—the name's Jared—and I'm damned if I'm going to act differently to what I feel in here—' he hit his chest savagely '—because you might put the wrong motives on it. You're going to have to learn to trust me; it's as simple as that.'

And then he closed the door on her shocked face.

CHAPTER TEN

HENRIETTA finally got up three days later. She had been amazed on the morning of her conversation with Jared when she had tried to make it to the bathroom alone and found her legs simply weren't up to the task, but the next forty-eight hours had seen a steady improvement. The enforced inactivity had given her plenty of time to think too—in between long bouts of dreamless sleep—but she was no nearer in her search for wisdom about what to *do* when she went down for breakfast that morning.

And since Jared had stated his intentions so clearly he had kept a very definite distance from her. Not in a cold, aloof way, she reassured herself as she tottered somewhat unsteadily into the breakfast room, but, nevertheless, the dissociation was not something she had imagined.

And her reaction to it confused her still more. She wanted to fling herself on him every time she saw him, devour him, eat him alive, and instead she had retreated into a tight little shell of her own making. A lonely, painful, *horrible* little shell.

The breakfast room was empty—Jared had clearly been and gone, and she assumed he had already left for his meeting in London that he had told her about the night before.

It was a beautiful August day; the sun was high in a cloudless blue sky and the scents of summer were heavy in the still air as she wandered out into the garden after a light breakfast of toast and orange juice, intending to take a few breaths of the intoxicating sunshine before settling herself down with a book she was reading.

Jared's gardener had got into the habit over the last week of exercising Murphy in the fields adjacent to Fotheringham, his benevolence prompted less by kindness and more by protection for his flowerbeds—Murphy had created havoc the first morning when he was bored—so Henrietta was quite alone, and after strolling down to a quiet bower in a curve of the lawn she sat, half hidden, on the little sun-warmed bench it boasted.

She heard Jared and Murphy before she saw them, and by the time they came within sight of her leafy retreat—where she could see out and remain unseen—she had realised Murphy had completely taken Jared to his heart. The two of them were engaged in a crazy game of tug of war with a massive chunky stick, and from the deep joyous woofs from Murphy, and the laughing, rough endearments from Jared, Henrietta knew it wasn't the first time they had enjoyed themselves in that way.

What was she doing comparing Jared with Melvyn for even the faintest moment?

She sat pole-axed, her heart thudding and her ears ringing as the blood surged hotly through her veins. Would Melvyn have ever shown affection to an animal like that, especially one that had a hold on her heart? Melvyn would have regarded Murphy as a threat, a rival, something that would dilute the feeling she had for him.

She closed her eyes, the sight of Jared and Murphy as they made their way back to the house too poignant as she realised how stupid, how criminally *blind* she had been.

And would Melvyn have raced Murphy to the veterinary surgery at some considerable risk to himself? Would he have even searched for him in the first place? And the commission Jared had put her forward for, the way he had off-loaded a good proportion of his work commitments abroad so he could spend more time in England—would Melvyn have done *any* of that?

Melvyn's sense of self-worth had been built on her degradation, her debasement; there had been no sacrifice in his feeling for her—until those last moments—rather a desire to subjugate and manipulate. *And Jared wasn't like that.* She sagged back against the warm wood as the wonder of it overwhelmed her.

She could wait weeks or months—even years—to let life confirm to her what she already knew, or she could get out there and *live* it at the side of the man she loved. And she did love Jared, more than she had ever fully admitted to herself until right at this moment. And in loving him she could forgive Melvyn—forgive him and thank him for the precious gift of life he had given her at the very end; it was the memory she had to lift above all the others.

'Henrietta?' She came out of the bubble as Jared called her, his voice sharp and concerned, and when Murphy's astute nose found her even before she had roused herself to answer him she knew a moment's fear at Jared's tone. But it was Jared speaking, not Melvyn, and it made all the difference, she told herself steadily.

'I'm here.' She stepped out of the shaded idyll into the bright, searching light of the morning, and saw him—tall and dark and so, so handsome—striding anxiously across the clear expanse of bowling-green-smooth lawn.

'We couldn't find you.' He forced a light smile but she had seen the darkness in the brilliant eyes and it swept away the last of her inhibitions and doubts. He *cared* as well as loved.

'I'm not going anywhere,' she said softly. She didn't want to waste another day, another hour of this precious gift called love. 'I've everything I want right here.'

For a moment Jared stared blankly at her, his eyes searching her face, and she could almost see the razor-sharp, perceptive brain analysing whether he had got it wrong.

'I've been stupid, Jared,' she said with trembling boldness. 'I had made up my mind that I wanted no attachments, no complications in my life because then I could be safe and nothing could hurt me. But if I lose you nothing could be worse than that. I love you and I trust you, and it really is as simple as that, isn't it?'

He stared at her for one more endless moment and then pulled her into him with a groan that said far more than any words could have done.

He crushed her lips in an agony of relief, moulding her into the hard shape of him as desire flared hot and fierce between them and they clung together as one.

'You'll marry me?' he growled urgently. 'Soon?'

'As soon as you want,' she whispered lovingly, looking up into his dark face and baring her soul. 'As soon as you want, my love.'

His mouth covered her face in little burning kisses and her head fell back languorously, the pure smooth line of her exposed throat his for the taking. 'I adore you, my darling, you know that, don't you?' he muttered against the silky softness of her skin. 'You are my sun, moon and stars, the reason for my next breath, my own sweet love—'

He stopped abruptly, and immediately, with an intuition born of her love, Henrietta reached up and took his face in her hands, stroking the rough cheeks with her thumbs as she said, 'Don't stop; I want you to say it all. You're mine and I'm yours; I'm not afraid any more.'

His mouth captured hers again, his tongue firing a response that made her arch against him as his hands swept over her possessively. She could feel the hard, pulsing evidence of his own passion against her body as they stood locked together, but she welcomed the silent declaration with a hunger that matched his own. He shifted her slightly in his arms, curving her into him as though he was staking a claim, the movement almost primitive, and she trembled at the hard power in the big male body.

'We're going to do this right, Henrietta,' he murmured softly against her mouth, 'but I don't think I can wait until we arrange a white wedding.'

'I don't want a white wedding, I just want you,' she said with brazen truthfulness.

'How much do you want me? Special licence much?'

'Special licence sounds lovely,' she said with transparent delight. A quiet wedding with the absolute minimum of furore and fuss couldn't be more different from the flamboyant, orange-blossom extravaganza she had shared with Melvyn, and that was just the way she wanted it. And one thing was for sure—her mother and David would drop everything once they knew whom she was marrying.

'And then a month or two somewhere hot and very, very secluded,' Jared said throatily. 'A desert island, perhaps, where we needn't bother

to wear clothes the whole time and I can do all
the things to you I've been dreaming about for
the last few months.'

'Have you?' Henrietta shivered in delicious
anticipation.

'Have I?' he echoed wryly, putting her from
him slightly as he devoured her with his eyes.
'Oh, lady, you'll never know.'

'I...I'm not very experienced.' Henrietta was
suddenly seized with the worry that he was expecting some *femme fatale*. 'Melvyn was my
first lover and he wasn't very...adventurous.'

'I am,' Jared told her with unrepentant satisfaction. 'And I've got the feeling there's an au-
dacious hussy in this delectable body just waiting to be let loose.'

Henrietta giggled. She felt light-headed,
giddy, wild even with the wonder and amazement of what she had done, but there were no
regrets, not one. Just a deep, abiding thankful-
ness that she had finally seen what her heart had
been trying to show her for months.

'I love you.' She was suddenly touchingly serious. 'More than I could ever have imagined
loving anyone.'

Jared looked down at her, his blue eyes narrowed against the white sunlight and his hard

square jaw firm and uncompromising. And then his face was wreathed in a smile, his rare smile that was for her alone as he lifted her right off her feet so her hands clung tightly round his neck. 'And I love you,' he murmured against her lips, 'every single little part of you, and I'm going to prove it to you for the rest of our lives.'

'Starting now?' Henrietta teased blissfully.

'Starting now,' he agreed, gathering her even closer to his heart, his powerfully muscled body causing her breath to catch in her throat and a sudden fierce passion to burn with a joyous abandonment that told her the years ahead were going to be overwhelmingly precious. Years filled with love and laughter, giving and receiving, years when the fruit of their love—children and grandchildren—would be cherished and held dear, and in their turn perpetuate the gift.

And so it proved.

MILLS & BOON® PUBLISH EIGHT
LARGE PRINT TITLES A MONTH.
THESE ARE THE EIGHT TITLES
FOR OCTOBER 1999

HAVING HIS BABIES
Lindsay Armstrong

THE MARRIAGE QUEST
Helen Brooks

THE SECRET MISTRESS
Emma Darcy

LOVER BY DECEPTION
Penny Jordan

ONE HUSBAND REQUIRED!
Sharon Kendrick

LONE STAR BABY
Debbie Macomber

THE TYCOON'S BABY
Leigh Michaels

A NINE-TO-FIVE AFFAIR
Jessica Steele

MILLS & BOON® PUBLISH EIGHT
LARGE PRINT TITLES A MONTH.
THESE ARE THE EIGHT TITLES
FOR NOVEMBER 1999

A HUSBAND OF CONVENIENCE
Jacqueline Baird

THE MOTHER OF HIS CHILD
Sandra Field

THE BABY CLAIM
Catherine George

FARELLI'S WIFE
Lucy Gordon

SHOTGUN BRIDEGROOM
Day Leclaire

THE BLACKMAILED BRIDEGROOM
Miranda Lee

THE MISTRESS BRIDE
Michelle Reid

UNDERCOVER FIANCÉE
Rebecca Winters

MILLS & BOON®

Makes any time special™

308381

Books should be returned on or before the
last date stamped below.

	2 8 JAN 1986	2 0 OCT 1990
13. MAY 03 92		13 NOV 1990
	- 2 APR 1986	
10. SEP 03 71		15. OCT 91
-9. FEB 84 73	2 3 AUG 1986	2 0 NOV 1991
27 JUN 1984	- 7 NOV 1986	
1 5 DEC 1984	2 4 JAN 1987	1 6 DEC 1991
1 8 JAN 1985	3 1 JUL 1987	
27 APR 1985	1 7 MAR 1988	2 9 JAN 1992
3 0 JUL 1985	SEP 88 2 6	
	- 5 NOV 1988	
- 9 OCT 1985	19 DEC 1988	9 MAR 1992
	- 3 FEB 1989	
-7 NOV 1985	- 6 OCT 1989	21. APR 92
21 DEC 1985	-7 APR 1990	12 OC 94 1994
		- 3 OCT 1995

NORTH EAST of SCOTLAND LIBRARY SERVICE
14 Crown Terrace, Aberdeen
